THE TRIAL OF MILTIADES

THE CAPTURE OF MILETOS

by

Francis Mace

Contents

The Trial of Miltiades

Reviews for The Trial of Miltiades:

***** proper use of fiction   8th May 2017

This fine novel looks behind the detail of certain phases of Athenian life (in 5th Century BCE), illuminating and enlivening them, without falsifying anything with the freedoms of fiction. Fiction is here doing its proper job, and is at the service of an account of reality which was, one is convinced, experienced; but which has not before now been put into written words.

D. F. Girardet de L'isle

***** Intriguing   By a customer on 20th May 2017

A work of special significance, giving an unusual and interesting opportunity…and insight into the workings and thoughts of the wealthy populace and their legal system at that time with great historical accuracy. A most enjoyable read.

Preface

Of Miltiades' trial, it is too early to assess the repercussions. On his return to Athens (Spring 493BCE), he has been prosecuted on a charge of tyranny in the Chersonese, a former Athenian colony.

His daughter Elpinike finds herself cast in roles both divine and semi-scandalous. Both she and her father are outsiders, if less so than their enemies imply.

The prosecution's case is reasonable and specious. Meanwhile Miltiades seems an unlikely defender of the democratic city and her values.

There's a kind of Tom and Viv (or Perikles-Aspasia) scenario, Elpinike having worked with her father on his speech.

From a fevered city and international crisis, an olive grove near the Sacred Way provides a haven…at least for the younger daughter, Kallidike.

Chapter 1

-Yes,- said Elpinike, who would have been exasperated
were there any point in it. -I've taught him to read and
write, and play the lyre. I don't know why it should
seem such an issue. It's a matter for me, I would have
thought - and the slave.- They were perhaps the last
words she would ever speak to her former friends.

To see those people is my duty, was a saying I
carried through part of the initiation with me last
autumn at Eleusis. I need nominal friends of my own
class to bore and ostracise me every day (yes the verb's
correctly chosen - you'd be surprised - but perhaps,
after all, you've been in such scenarios yourself), and if
their company makes me physically ill and harms my
psyche - that's acceptable - indeed the unacceptable
is very acceptable. (*Elpinikean irony* is a phrase that
came into vogue lately and will remain there for - oh,
some millennia, or so I imagine. 'It's women like her
who get remembered.' No doubt you've heard such
remarks.)

'You don't break with folks like that, of the highest
character and class, unless there's something wrong
with you, and you're degenerate,' my father explained
to me, on becoming aware of my newly evolved stance.

The goddesses led me on at Eleusis, and I remain in
surprising psychic territory. They seemed to take
delight in eroding my seriousness. But you know what
will happen, I said to them.

Oh yes, we've seen the fields of asphodel; a distressed Demeter searching for her daughter…and their reunion, there at Eleusis.

I was in a Demeter-like search for *myself.*

All praise to the two goddesses. And yet…well I'm still…for all their assistance and jokes…I don't think I'm quite sane, actually. The world is so *big*. It engulfs me when I step out of the house.

-I've been drawn into a lower sort of communion, and enjoyed it overmuch,- was one of the suggestions she threw in her sister Kallidike's direction.

-You've changed, no doubt,- her sister remarked without interrupting her spinning of some wool. –You have more reason than ever to be glad that we're protected and barricaded from the world.-

The hue and cry would come so close at times, it was prudent to place the palms of their hands over their ears. It wouldn't have benefitted them to hear the accusations in detail.

A few days later they were to move into the country at Lakiadai, three miles north of the city.

They went on foot, escorted by their brother. He was sober for the occasion. It's good exercise, they had all agreed.

-Better in some ways than kneading the dough,- Elpinike remarked.

The thought impressed itself on her: Even the dough looks different now I'm in trouble. It was as if everything in the universe had a similar dark message - something uncomplimentary about her.

Yes and I'm not listening.

Oh but I'll make you.

It's other people who turn the midday sky black. I could take them seriously. But I could borrow a grimace from Glaukothea. She's good at that - and quite shameless too. She has been practicing unacceptable looks from her childhood. It's one of the things she's most well-known for. Personally, I admire her. She feels that women in general are in for it. More so than most men? I've ask her. She may be right. I've assumed the grimaces to predate her theories by some years. But do they really? I can't be sure. Children can think, and have the advantage of not being drunk. Anyway, she may have had a previous life, which taught her a lot. (See the works of Pythagoras. I think they can be still found in the temple at Olympia, where he placed them on his way to Italy.)

These were dangerous days for Parmeno himself. It may not be wise to give hope to a slave who has never experienced it. It might plunge him into its opposite, rendering intolerable scenarios and demands to which he had grown resigned.

Oh, but the music... How he loved even quite simple syntheses and sequences of notes, as they each held a lyre, and the value of their sounds seemed more than doubled. The gods themselves seemed amazed by the beauty of what they could achieve, though in their humility the pair of them would concede it was probably nothing special in comparison with the more technically demanding work of professional musicians.

You wouldn't have thought Elpinike in some sort of turmoil, to look at her. But often she would lie on her bed by day, without moving.

–I'm a bit pre-occupied, Kallidike,- she said to her fifteen year old sister one midsummer day.

-You're preoccupied with lying down like this, and cuddling the blankets - or holding your head between your hands?-

-Yes, I'm busy lying down. By my bed you'll see the papyrus you've been waiting for. Read it, if you want. I can't complete it. Or maybe it contains as much as I wanted to say, on father's trial. I don't feel moved to add anything to Cleainetos' speech. I could attempt some sort of exordium, but it would be largely made up. I've forgotten so much... If there's something important you recall, and that I've left out - oh - put it in yourself. I'm really thrown and wrecked.-

-Yet you teach Parmeno.-

-He helps me. I hardly know how.-

Her sister held her hand, felt her forehead, looked in cautious enquiry into her eyes, and seemed puzzled. – You've survived your social death,- she announced.

-Oh it's remarkable, I know,- said Elpinike. – *Charin toisi theoisi* - thanks to the gods. But it's just a reprieve. My body hasn't caught up with what my mind knows. Nor has my mind yet caught up with itself.-

Chapter 2

The talk about Miltiades' and his youngest son's narrow
escape from the Phoenician fleet had taken an
unexpected twist; turned into the basis of innuendos and
disturbing comments. People spoke knowingly of
Kimon's loving reunion with his sister. They were seen
to embrace at Phalerum, on Kimon's climbing down the
ladder from his trireme, into the shallow water. (This
was no harbour, just a beach for drawing up the ships.)
She got wet (so it was said) having gone into the sea to
meet him. Between her legs you mean? men would ask
in drunken exchanges on the subject. That her get-
togethers with her half-brother were over-warm was a
common assumption among the slaves; and the stories
of incest spread like a forest fire through a city hungry
for news about high class people. Were the scandal-
mongers a happy alliance of the good and the evil?
That tended to be her reluctant conclusion, or at least
impression.

Soon after Miltiades' return, came the trial; and
Elpinike was working on documents relating to it when,
without her knowledge, the scandal was rife all around
her. Her belated enlightenment by what felt like the
pouring of darkness into her innocent soul from a world
about which her own thoughts were less than
complimentary, seemed to paralyse her hand as she
tried to continue the work. Yet maybe after all she was

right, that by now it was fairly complete, or as much so as she could make it.

Chapter 3

Is life destined to lack meaningful destiny?

Pausing in her work one day she had reflected, concerning the Medes: They'll burn our temples and explain why they were right to do so...

It may be as if we never existed. When we're hundreds of miles from here, on the banks of the Euphrates or wherever, we can ask ourselves how Athenian we feel... Our history is to be forgotten. It won't even be a drop in the ocean of imperial time. They'll educate us to consider developments here an irrelevance, or worse. It's not a story they will want to hear told. Our identities are not the recommended sort.

We need records of free thought, free human souls. Maybe in thousands of years, cracks will emerge in the barbarian power, fissures where light can get through...

None of our poets is thought to equal Homer. Our prose is...prosaic. But there is some notion of life being viewed differently, so you could get things from us you couldn't get from the earlier writers...or perhaps from people of later times. How broad is the band of time in which we are ourselves? It might be insufficient to amount to anything much. There may be little for us after all to contribute...

Chapter 4

She thanked the gods that she had been allowed more or less to complete the work before tales of her bad reputation got through to her. Perhaps after all she would still have been able to write, despite being too often forced to dwell on the way others' thoughts were dwelling on her. But the delay in the arrival of the burden had surely been very much to her advantage.

Ironically, she couldn't spend that much time with Kimon. She was with him in others' thoughts even as the prospect and experience of lengthy absences from him really came home to her. Young men didn't stay at home with their sisters; at least, not for long. At fourteen, he had to show he could do more than drink wine and sleep with her. He might have spent more time with her, but for the loss of their eldest brother. *He* was doing fine - Metiochos was arguably better off than anyone in the family, or in the city, for that matter. But (one might almost say *for* here) he was far away, and it would be Kimon whom the family would look to, to continue the tradition of public service and military leadership, so well represented by Miltiades himself.

The person she relied on most was perhaps Kallidike, her junior by two years. Of her step-mother, Hegesipyle, she was wary. The mother of Kimon and Kallidike would have you conclude from her demeanour and way of life that she was no barbarian. This Thracian princess wanted you to know that there was nothing in her values or conduct that would lend support to the common belief that people of her race were rather wild and either lacking in self-control or self-controlled in a way that would serve and prioritise Dionysian impulses and desires. Elpinike felt (or felt that she was expected to feel) that she let her step-mother down by representing what she was determined to repudiate. How far she herself resembled in character her own mother - Hegesipyle's sister - who had died within a few hours of giving birth to her, she didn't know.

Chapter 5

Kallidike heard voices as she was walking near the vineyard. Her hand tightened on the papyrus roll her sister had just given her. Looking along the rows of trees supporting the vines she saw Kimon talking to some slaves. She dared herself to go and join them; and listened as the slaves spoke of their anxieties and aspirations. –Tell us if you have any problems. We don't want you all committing suicide,- said the fifteen year old girl, by way of self-reintroduction. -You know fine well you can escape whenever you should choose.-

–Where would we want to escape to?- said Getas, the oldest of the group.

–To a worse life, of course!- said resigned young Sosias. –Well, you don't keep us chained up,- he remarked to Kimon. The men felt a certain unspoken gratitude for how they were treated. They were free both from the troubles of maltreated slaves, and the perils of the citizenry. These labourers would never experience the burdens of high status. It was the true Athenians who bore the brunt of the highest expectations. They would demand little from others as they faced the spears of the enemy.

-Tell us if *you* have any problems,- said Getas to Kimon.

-You know what eminence is - or can guess, perhaps,- said the fourteen year old Kimon.

-It is to be lower than the Titans of Tartarus,- said Kallidike, cheering them up with a smile. —Though I'm personally hardly the centre of the social storm, I'm obviously affected by it.-

-How do you cope with the difficult aspects of your position?- said Getas. —Some are driven to drink...-

-That hasn't happened to me,- said Kimon.

-The wine has affected his memory,- Kallidike explained.

There was much more that Kallidike might have said, that seemed rather improper to go into in detail in speaking to the slaves. Not that the latter were quite unaware of it anyway...in this place where aspirations were not only high but less clearly defined than elsewhere. Here, aspiration itself was a sort of creativity, a fact which made life more exciting no doubt but also more nerve-wracking.

Some men would pray: Dionysos, set us free from the double trouble we face: the trouble of the problematical nature of masculinity, and the trouble of its twisted and more sinister theoretical aspects, as evolved by civilisation.

What is it doing to me, this culture? We have all of us no doubt - all in this society of ours - asked ourselves that question. What inhuman thing is it turning me into? Must I become through conformism something I don't like, something detested, and rightly so, by men and by gods?

Don't be taken in for a moment by the nonsense the world is trying to teach you...

At parties, many high class men wear female attire. Some keep their beards - ironically; to heighten the sense of a disconcerting clash, as of cymbals associated with followers of Bacchus; and to make all the easier their return to 'normal' life.

An aristocrat may not be able to say: I'm somebody! without incurring a rather pitying derision. To earn special respect he would need to be a great man. But if he's a great man, and wins a thousand victories through much suffering and risk to life and limb, and then makes some blunder, imparting 'good advice' which on re-analysis turns out to be also flawed and poor, he must face the disapproval of the citizen assembly, perhaps of the courts and their (predominantly peasant) juries. He is a bad man! He was never trustworthy! Why is he drinking so much! He's self-indulgent! He's not one of us! He's a pampered aristocrat! Let's get rid of him! So off he goes into exile. But maybe he doesn't drink too much after all. Maybe he prefers the ladies' clothes, having realised that, in his masculinity, he could only take so much.

Some acknowledgment of such considerations seemed to guide Getas as he said to Kimon and his sister: -Well - we'll look after you. We won't treat you as all those superior people do - your fellow citizens.-

-Thanks,- said Kallidike, before walking away.

She made for the olive grove; and her favourite tree therein. Now for some light reading, she said to herself. She climbed up easily enough to sit near the junction of a branch and the trunk of the ancient tree. It's not that far to the ground from here, so if the god shakes the earth, I won't have far to fall. Anyway I can hold onto some foliage. The tree has been here hundreds of years and is likely to remain quite steady.

She couldn't see the Sacred Way from where she was, and it was consoling to feel that she probably couldn't be seen from there, by people going along it.

Elpinike had accused her more than once of wanting to be like Nausikaa, or some other character in Homer's Phaiakia. If Sappho were writing today, opined Elpinike, she would have been an historian as well as a poet. Kallidike conceded that she was unwilling to dwell on the sinister powers that seemed about to overwhelm their world. She seemed to imagine that by not thinking about them she kept them at bay.

She partly unrolled the papyrus on Miltiades' trial, which had taken place almost exactly two months before. Yes, it was an event of spring, that queer spring in which they fined the poet, Phrynichos, for his play about the fall of Miletos.

She settled down to read.

She found that, as usual, her sister had revealed her own viewpoint. She seemed to seek a synthesis of the individual perspective she was used to adopting in poetry, with a more impersonal approach, like that of the historian Hecataeus of Miletos.

Kimon was displaying his weaker side on the day. He had had so much wine that you couldn't sit him where he would be conspicuous. He not only *was* drunk, he looked it too. So it was decided Kallidike and Glaukothea should sit with him in comparative obscurity, a few rows from the front, to keep an eye on him.

The younger and elder sister would be spoken of in Cleainetos' speech for the prosecution as, unlike Elpinike, absent from the proceedings. It was a sign of disrespect that they were spoken of by name. It was startling to Kallidike to hear of her supposed absence. Though no great theorist on the nature of things, it was difficult not to view the fact that she could hear him say she wasn't there as firm evidence of her presence.

Kallidike imagined some future historian as specialising in misapprehensions, mistakes, delusions and misleading ideas.

Elpinike...you can be eccentric and unusual in your comments... You have a nonchalance that comes in the aftermath of father's success. At times this reads like a private diary, unmeant for anyone else's perusal... Let me see... It looks ragged at first, and the beginning is not like a beginning. It's as if one were reading notes. She's got no discretion, and will tell you things you're not supposed to know.

What happens to the present, when it's no longer the present? Where does it go? It's like those words I've just spoken.

Chapter 6

The text in Kallidike's hands was as follows:

The Trial of Miltiades

The author - Elpinike, seventeen year old daughter of
the defendant - will write of herself in the third person,
unless in such recollected thoughts as may include the
odd *ego, eme, emou,* or *emoi.* After all, to you I'm
'she', *n'est ce pas?* Certainly not 'I'.

The trial takes place in the southern court of the
agora, in the archonship of Pythocritos. His term of
office still has a few more months to run. The judge,
Themistokles, is archon-designate and although the
official year won't begin until midsummer, his prestige
is almost as high as anyone's; his influence the more
significant because of his electoral success.

To Elpinike's right sits the defendant himself, her
father. To their left, extending before them in a big
concave crescent, are the five hundred and one jurors.
Beyond the area in front, where the defendant will
speak, extends the agora with its market stalls, shrines,
vividly painted statues, and various colonnaded
buildings. At the centre of the concavity is
Themistokles with his assistants; while beyond them at
the farther end, are the prosecutor and his supporters.
Placed a little forward from the front row of benches,
and interrupting its continuity, the well-made chairs of

the judge and his colleagues help to confirm their special role and status.

'I'm as exposed to the public as you,' Miltiades has joked with Elpinike. He looks around to find a certain conclusion confirmed. 'You're their Aphrodite and an extra special reason to attend,' he says. 'Even my enemies fall in love with you. But... Well how do you think *I* feel?' He makes her laugh with his complaints, and puts her at ease by claiming not to be so himself. Meanwhile Elpinike retains such hope as amply justifies her name. This is partly because Aristeides has done what he can to reassure her, but also because she finds it difficult to imagine, her father having been of high status for so long, that he can suddenly lose it like some character in tragedy.

As the prosecution gets going, she reflects: If my father is really not in too much danger, I may enjoy almost shamelessly the pleasure of hearing him called a tyrant.

How sly his enemies look - Cleainetos, the speaker, most of all. Their faces seem closed like fists gripping nothing. The loyalties of this Cleainetos are considered to be suspect. This doesn't have to matter too much, as one can address the points he raises on their merits without constantly insinuating that his motives are corrupt. If they are corrupt, a good legal point is still that, if he can make it. But there is the rumour that he has links with the Alkmaionidai family, which is more than ever like the goaded bear in some of the Artemis myths. If they want to make Miltiades feel isolated, it's what they already seem to be themselves. But much is unclear; the very nature of Athens, not established.

Perhaps the Alkmaionidai are not exiles in their own home city after all. It is indeed easy to argue that few citizens are more eligible to be described as outsiders than Miltiades. Yes, easy to say that, and that he is an outsider who definitely belongs here...as criminals certainly do belong, in a sense. Who has a truer and deeper feeling of belonging, than criminals...at their trial? If you are in any other scenario, you may well in your humility defer to others and allow them priority of attention. But the one standing trial is definitely of special importance. Not that this was the kind of importance or centrality that Miltiades was hoping for when returning from abroad last month. These Athenians don't take long to mount a legal case...

These half-sentences half amuse her: -If the anti-tyrant legislation is to mean anything...; and, - Miltiades' power in the Chersonese deriving from Hippias, whose tyrannical rule here has left such bitter memories...-

Well, what a *cause celebre!* How wide and varied the *corona* - the throng of people outside the court who are looking over the barrier to see and hear what happens. There are men and women here from every part of Attica, and many too from elsewhere; Corinthians, Thessalians, envoys of the kings of Sparta...

Cleainetos paces a few moments in silence. He clears his throat; turns again to face the jury. The look in his eyes and way his chin and brow seem to come fractionally closer to each other help to show that he still feels well-prepared. Now his every word is a few thousand message-bearing arrows, finding simultaneously many targets.

-He seems to have thought, 'In this strange place' (the stranger for the fact that he was there) 'I can do as I please. Being so far from home, an exotic aura should protect my reputation.' May I remind you, Miltiades - we're talking about an Athenian colony and lands thereto assimilated. In theory - and however your misrule led to revised expectations - they were subject to our laws...-

She cautiously keeps an ear on the trend of the speech, to see if any surprises are sprung. Meanwhile she recites to herself verses from the *Iliad*, which she finds a welcome counterpoint. Lines of her choosing include some about an arrow on its way from Pandarus' bow to Menelaus. She has often read to her sister this account of how Athena alters the course of the missile, as by wafting her hand a woman may suddenly deflect a stinging insect on its way to her child. The arrow almost harmlessly buries itself in Menelaus' belt and clothing. But there is some fear of poison, and the doctor prudently sucks at the wound in an effort to clean it.

Our political life doesn't contain any venom, of course...

Oh yes, the scenario in the Chersonese, six years before I was born... The governor, Stesagoras (my father's elder brother) is approached in the Town Hall by a man claiming to be a deserter from the enemy city of Lampsakos...

Elpinike imagines explaining this to someone whom she has yet to meet. The person lacks any off-putting or inhibiting qualities. You don't have to work hard to modulate what you say to them, to avoid giving offence. Sometimes (so she suggests to herself) to meet some significant friend, you first have to imagine them. She puts in more detail, in her mind's voice, than the prosecution feels the need to expound. -'I'll join your side,' the man tells Stesagoras, who, smiling, comes near to offer his hand in welcome. Taking one of the axes down from the wall, the Lampsakene kills him with a single blow. The consequent disorder and confusion in the colony encourage the Lampsakenes, who, crossing the strait in their warships, attack and plunder, destroying crops and burning farms. Learning of what is going on, Hippias sends my father to sort things out.

She attends more carefully. Can the speaker begin to explain why a fatal wave of indignation should arise?

–The arrival of the defendant in Sestos brings little reassurance. He's there, and he's not there, so to speak. Having made for Stesagoras' former home, he keeps himself to himself. Is he hoping to appear weak?- wonders Kleainetos. –If so, he succeeds.

-Many chieftains of the region travel to the house to offer condolences. Their welcome is warm in its way, for they are arrested and thrown into prison. It's the mark of a character like his, gentlemen, not to trust even his friends. As those nobles sit in their chains, he feels that much is set to rights, his power secure. The Lampsakenes are setting up a base at the western end of the peninsula, and yes, he *will* get round to responding. 'But after all, *they* are only his enemies,' his subjects remark to each other. His lesson in crime and injustice has made a deep impression on the Thracians. 'Seek civilised friends!' - is a saying of long standing among them, and alludes ironically to this representative of our city.

-It's odd how he goes on about the founder of the colony, Miltiades son of Kypselos. We admit of course the family connection. But a comparison of character between the son of Kimon and the son of Kypselos would tend to strengthen the case against the former.-

Elpinike shakes her head impatiently. I *am* biased...

The story, from a few generations back, of my family's first involvement with the Chersonese... Many in the audience are likely to be telling it to themselves, or reconsidering it, at this moment. It may perhaps be more helpful to my father, than Cleainetos seems to believe.

Chapter 7

She sees herself as a young girl, in the house on the
Areopagos. Her step-mother pauses in work at the
loom. It's a natural and obvious fact, my being here, an
eight year old girl, with Hegesipyle. Childhood is so
real even when past; and later life can seem somehow
arbitrary. It's only one of millions of possible threads
of fate; or it's no thread at all but seems to happen just
anyhow. The disorientation includes a sense of
freedom. Yes I'm so free I can move into the past. In
thought I'm in a place that feels good. It seems to smell
all the more pleasant for not being redolent of anything
at all.

Elpinike has been speaking of the family link with
the Chersonese, a land which she herself has yet to see.
–My friends are puzzled as to how we first got involved
in the region. I haven't been able to explain.-

-Oh it's to do with the elder son of your great
grandmother,– said Hegesipyle. –You know that
Praxithea had a son called Kimon - who was your
father's father. But Kimon was the offspring of her
second marriage. By her earlier marriage, to a man of
Corinthian origin named Kypselos, she already had a
son: Miltiades. This elder Miltiades, the son of
Kypselos, and half-brother of Kimon, was the first
Athenian governor of the Chersonese.-

Hegesipyle speaks comparatively slowly. Her
Greek is formal and studied. The women are more

careful than the men, with the language, knowing theirs
is the main responsibility to teach new generations to
speak. But Hegesipyle is more self-consciously correct,
Greek not being her mother tongue. In fact she has
taken a long time (much longer than a child would
need) to learn to speak the language of Athens. Her
learning has depended far less on her husband (though
they do sometimes spend time with each other) than on
several of his female relatives and some servants.

Elpinike sits on the stool by the loom as Hegesipyle
remains standing there, as if ready to resume work. -It
may be an obvious place for Athenians to settle,- said
the girl. We want foodstuffs to reach us via the Black
Sea. But why should the elder Miltiades have played so
eminent a role in that far away land?-

-A few generations ago,- says Hegesipyle, -when
the son of Kypselos was in his thirties, the peoples of
the Chersonese were experiencing military pressure
from neighbouring tribes. Troubled by fears of the
imminent eclipse of their nation, princes of the
Dolonkoi - the chief tribe of the Chersonese -
travelled to Greece. They came to Delphi to consult the
oracle. We need a leader to protect us, they said to the
officials of the shrine. Who should it be? The response
of the priestess was as follows: The first to offer you
hospitality as you walk away from the shrine is the
person you are looking for.

-For some miles, as they proceeded along the Sacred
Way, no one invited them in. It was a habit of Miltiades
son of Kypselos, at evening, to sit outside his house,
which overlooks that road.-

-You mean our own house - the one at Lakiadai?-
asks Elpinike.

-It didn't know you, or me... But yes, the same
house. - He liked to sit there, in the open air, facing
north, and some of his neighbours observed, 'It's pretty
obvious that he prefers to face away from the city.'
'Hope and new life...' he had lately taken to saying
sardonically in their hearing, while looking towards the
north. His manner seemed to make of the words a back-
handed insult to Peisistratos, then at last (to all
appearances) securely in power. (In truth the tyrant
would be toppled a few months later and the long
apparently interminable period of his rule wasn't to
begin for another decade or so).-

    -This is a tale of...very long ago,- Elpinike says.

    -Well...we're looking at a time, about five or six
years before the birth of your father. It really can seem
a very long time ago, partly because of the great
changes that have taken place since. In the period of
which I speak, Croesus was the confident king of Lydia,
and the Persians had yet to threaten either him or the
cities of Ionia.-

    -But please, resume your story of the son of
Kypselos. I think I have an idea of what's likely to
happen next!-

    -As they walked along the Sacred Way, the princes
of the Dolonkoi effectively proclaimed, by their richly
coloured clothes, and spears of unfamiliar type, that
they were not local men - indeed, that they were not
Hellenic. Seeing the princes approach, Miltiades felt he
liked them. They seemed refreshingly remote from -
even nobly ignorant of - dark intrigue such as that
which made the city less and less pleasant to him.-

    -He asked them in,- Elpinike guessed.

-Yes. Rarely, I suppose, has the relation of host and guest appeared more meaningful! How amazed Miltiades must have felt, to learn that his decision to entertain some passers-by, should turn out to confer on him the character of guardian of their nation. He broached the subject of a colony with some sensitivity, unsure how they might feel about foreigners as it were invading, with whatever friendly intentions. But they assured him how much they would value, and be grateful for, a strong contingent of Athenian soldiers to strengthen their defences. Should they bring their families and become permanent settlers, so much the better.

-'I'll speak to the Delphic officials to verify what you say about the oracle,' said Miltiades. 'Then I'll have to do something I haven't done for a while - that is, speak to the tyrant of this land. You may have heard that Peisistratos and I don't get on. But if I'm to arrange for the foundation of a colony, I'll need his co-operation. However, his desire to get rid of me and of as many people as possible who agree with me in matters of politics, is so intense that I expect he'll practically order me to go ahead with this scheme.'

-Miltiades was correct in his assessment of how Peisistratos would respond. The men were selected, and soon the city of Lampsakos was disappointed to find, facing it across the strait, a formidable new colony of people from here. Miltiades fulfilled his duties, keeping back the enemies of the Dolonkoi and maintaining order...-

Chapter 8

A certain fear of Cleainetos reasserting itself both with
and against her will, Elpinike resumes her scrutiny of
his words. It disconcerts her to look back on her
conversation with Hegesipyle. It was so warmly
apparent to me, just now. Am I to question its
authenticity on the grounds that the past is unreal? I
would prefer to speculate on parallel realities, than to
dismiss experience as rendered untrue by the effects of
time. Well, at least I know this trial to be authentic.
For a few moments she grips the wood of the bench she
is sitting on, and looks around to receive the present
reality of the audience.

   -I have no reason to impugn the achievements of the
elder Miltiades,- Cleainetos is saying. -The local
people owe to him the wall across the neck of the
peninsula; the defeat of the Apsinthians... The war
against Lampsakos could not be won, perhaps; but he
made sure it was not lost. He justly receives heroic
honours. The games held in his name amount to a
celebration of the saviour of the region.

   -Apparently, the defendant wants you to feel that
prestige and a sort of magic passed to him from the son
of Kypselos. He seems to suggest that in receiving the
same name as the founder, he inherited a comparable
destiny.- (Here Cleainetos' look implies he expects to
find such disdain in others as he himself cannot but
share. If you're not disdainful yet, look at me. My

expression will show you how to react. If you are sensible and want to win approval, this is how to respond. If you don't, you're not a right-thinking citizen. We could be investigating you, soon, so be careful.) -'It's the most natural thing in the world for me to resemble the great man,' he seems to say.

-Miltiades, appraise matters less vainly. Let go, as quite useless, axioms which, although for long current in your tyrant's court, cannot be seen in a court of justice as other than the absurdities they always were. No one here - not even yourself, I suspect, in this place where the light of reason surely dawns for you at last - is impressed by your attempts to borrow someone else's destiny. No oracle ever backed you, as lord of the Chersonese. You're not the founder of the colony, reincarnated. The fact that your own life and that of the son of Kypselos were for many years going on simultaneously makes the idea particularly farcical. Indeed the claim was never made explicitly, for you and your friends knew it to be unacceptable even to Pythagoreans. Some thoughts indeed have a chance for a while if implied but never really expressed or examined. They may be accepted rather as we accept wordless music. And indeed music can mislead.-

(But couldn't they be a kind of spiritual twins, or something similar - my father and the son of Kypselos? Elpinike says to herself. I'm not saying they were, but the idea's not absurd.)

-The Delphic pronouncement we think you should focus on is not the one that concerns your illustrious relative, but the injunction *gnothi seauton,* know yourself.-

The speaker keeps looking to his own side for support and encouragement. The wind blows at his hair, which seems to be greying by the moment. He raises his voice, glances anxiously at the water-clock.

-Until recently, this man was regularly carried about in a litter. He kept a bodyguard of five hundred mercenaries - always on hand, in case anyone should mention something inconvenient or irritating, like law and justice.

-'There was little desire for democracy in the Chersonese,' Miltiades says. 'The mix of languages and customs would have made it hard to establish. What the people agreed in wanting was strong military leadership, which I provided.' But in a real crisis, don't take his prowess for granted, or imagine that he has any. During invasions by Scythian hordes, we see him withdrawing to an inland region of Thrace. 'I'll wait here,' he says to himself, 'until the migrations have passed and it's safe to go back.' So much for leadership, of any sort whatsoever.

-Miltiades owned a number of the Thracian gold mines. His supporters received a huge supply of treasure and gold coin. Bribery seemed to him much more useful than any sort of good government. The latter would seem to him dull, routine, boring... One way he got people on his side was to invite them to the parties he held in and around his house at Eion. Some of the most accomplished and expensive courtesans would attend. As the lascivious music played, men were heard to say, 'Only Miltiades can finance fun as exquisite as this!' His sober calculation - when he *was* sober - was that sound principles would dissolve amid the pleasures of Dionysos and Aphrodite.

-'If I've hurt the cause of democracy,' he says, 'it has been against my will, and merely through governing well.' A bad ruler, he suggests, may help his people by inducing in them a revolutionary fervour. 'That my own rule never had that effect is testimony to its mildness.' - In fact many complained, at least in private, of his misrule. They noted, but couldn't do anything about, his tendency to favour the wilder, Thracian element of the populace, over the Athenian. This favouritism was particularly apparent in his second term, when the constitution of Athens constituted an only too obvious challenge to what he stood for. He was most at ease with lackeys who knew little of democracy. People said at the time, 'You would think nothing much had changed in Athens and his old master, Hippias, were still in power.' To step into Miltiades' realm, was like stepping back in time. As laws and institutions evolved here, his regime began to look more and more *passé*.

-Look at his sneering face. He is laughing, but not only at us. He is laughing at you all, gentlemen. Consider your safety and remove this pest, obnoxious alike at home and abroad. Let the protection of our laws be denied him. Let him die, as he deserves, at the hands of some good citizen. Once he has been condemned, to kill him would of course be a blameless act, an acknowledged favour to us all. I believe songs would one day be composed in honour of such a benign assassination.

-Don't rest your eyes for long on Elpinike, this seventeen year old who has the misfortune to be his daughter. 'I'm just an ordinary man with a family to support,' he implies by bringing her before you. (It's surprising he hasn't brought Glaukothea, Kallidike and Kimon along too.) But don't let him make fools of you. Don't re-categorise him as a harmless private individual, as if a man's past were somehow divorced from his present and no strong evidence as to his nature and intentions. To deny what is going on - what his lusts and arrogance are impelling him towards - is essential to the plan. His dream is that none of you will know for sure what powerful forces he is gathering, and why, until the day he sets up a new tyranny here to replace the petty one which the Persians have just taken from him.

-When he promises to behave well in future, you are aware that every criminal does the same in similar circumstances. He expects you to use your imaginations and see his past as better than it was. Your duty, however, is to consider carefully the facts that we adduce, facts which his evasions and euphemisms cannot obscure or disguise. I pay you the compliment, gentlemen, of assuming that this disgrace to our commonwealth will soon lose the protection of our laws. Of all the crimes ever committed, his is perhaps the most well-known, public and undeniable.-

The speaker sits down. Something in his final tones suggests he expects applause from the *corona*. But it maintains a leaden silence. He tries not to look disappointed.

Themistokles, the presiding judge, has long curvy moustaches which like the rest of his wavy beard is nowhere grey, just brown and auburn. His wide intelligent eyes seem to take in the world with an eager delight. He often glances at Elpinike, apparently with considerable interest and pleasure. Perhaps his belief that Miltiades will be acquitted explains his sitting back and enjoying, in an easy-going manner, all the accusations being levelled at his political rival and colleague. At times it seems this is his idea of a holiday. As he occupies his ornate, high chair between the contending parties, he enjoys the proceedings as much, perhaps, as he might a play. Yes, he seems to be thinking, things are not going as badly as I had feared. Though no friend of Miltiades, Themistokles recognises his worth and courage, and admires the ways he has shown himself averse to Persian dominance.

Chapter 9

The sky is unusually dark when Cleainetos sits down. Conversations of members of jury and *corona* create a business-like hum; and, though you can sense the tension, no voices are being raised in anger. Elpinike and her father are discussing some unforeseen developments in the prosecution tactics, which require alterations and additions to his speech. -But really, there's little of importance that the preliminary hearing didn't prepare us for,- says Miltiades. -Well, what a sky is this?- he adds. -Have you ever seen it so grim?-

Not many moments later, when the defendant is asked by Themistokles to speak, the sun comes out. Miltiades' supporters smile at each other, cautiously under their brows. It is difficult not to feel encouraged by a sky which…well, maybe it is divine after all. At least, it seems to have its divine moments.

Miltiades rises and walks forward until he is midway along the semi-ellipse of jurors. Thus, as is expected and required, he positions himself quite close to Themistokles.

Despite the grizzled hair and the sunburnt, wrinkled features, the defendant is still a handsome man, and he knows it. He is impressive partly because he has no doubt of his ability to be so. Yet his manner is measured, careful, there is no arrogance. He has studied the knack of treating others as equals. He has imbibed already, not a moment too soon, something of the democratic ideology. After all like a well-practiced actor, he can show what he can do, and what he has to offer, rather than what the occasion itself can do to crush him, which so far at least, it apparently cannot. Indeed his former career imparts such confidence that to feign a few moments of gauche timidity seems prudent. -No one makes a better democrat than an old tyrant,- a number of people will approvingly agree, or at least suggest to each other, on that day.

I feel trapped in my own body, Elpinike reflects. I want to view the whole court coolly as a god might, from above. The sense of freedom she had felt during Cleainetos' speech is now worryingly absent. I've preferred listening to the prosecution. - There, she admits it. A sense of being trapped, oh yes, she is used to that, under her father's influence. It is odd how his positive qualities - and she is sure he has some - don't easily get through to her consciousness. Then again, if she becomes aware of them, they don't seem to bring her closer to the *eudaimonia*, the spiritual well-being, that she craves. She cannot feel grateful that, unlike so many fathers, he has decided to raise all his daughters. She draws in a deep breath. Oh yes, she thinks, though not with good grace, it's very possible that, were another man my father (she is looking more keenly now than before at the jurors) I'd be, not somehow constricted, but dead.

She is sitting near the water-clock, which awakens in her a desire to urinate, but she feels awkward about getting up and going to the nearest closet or quiet alleyway. She doesn't want to distract attention from her father's speech. It would be rude to walk out, as if in protest, while he is in full flow. As she is considering how bad it would look, his words seem to pulse within her, to the increasing of her need to relieve herself.

Chapter 10

In fact she does get her opportunity to relieve herself,
for as her father is just about to speak, everyone
becomes distracted by the sudden entry into the open
space of a rapid little, long-eared creature. The hare
begins darting about here and there in confusion. There
is a general release of tension, and some laughter, as
clerks of the court hunt the animal, with minimal
success. Elpinike rises and gets the barrier opened for
her by an official so that she can pass through the
corona. –No, I'm nobody,- she keeps assuring people
as she is being accused of being related to the accused.
The slave Timandra has dutifully opted to come with
her, so she is not alone in the throng. Officials in the
agora are quite willing to direct her to some safe place
where she can meditate, if she feels like it, on the
superiority, actual or imagined, of humans over other
animals while emptying her bladder. Having done this I
can stand in for Aphrodite with more equanimity, she
reflects.

Everyone seems to think the entry of the hare a sign
from the gods. No one will dare kill it because they
don't know what the creature is a sign *of.* After its
capture it is given to someone who says his son will
look after it and keep it as a pet. For all anyone knows
it may signify the city herself, so much in danger as she
is of becoming like an animal in a trap. A number of
seers are consulted, who agree that to harm the hare and

thus risk incurring the anger of Artemis would be very unwise and impious.

The attempts to catch the creature and the discussions, after it is caught, as to how the gods may want them to react to the possible sign, go on for some time.

While re-traversing the agora and making her way back to her place on the bench on the east side of the court, Elpinike is more concerned to follow her own train of thought than to scrutinise goings on around her.

Chapter 11

She contemplates a scene of a few days earlier in their olive grove at Lakiadai, where her father expressed a number of concerns which he has no intention of alluding to here.

   –What's the point of my sound defence, if sound it be, if there are powers at work that can skew the course of the trial?- he said impatiently to Aristeides, who sat before him in a bend of a twisted olive tree. Elpinike, who stood to Aristeides' left, noted his quiet smile, which seemed to suggest the view that Miltiades was prone to exaggeration, and giving vent to an understandable and as it were reasonable unreasonableness. –You know how Phrynichos was in for it last month for writing an anti-Persian play.-

   Aristeides and Elpinike felt invited to partake of a kind of grim theatricality.

   -If a poet has to pay a financial penalty for opposing Darius - well, they'll expect me to pay a graver one.- The addressee looked away from Miltiades and glanced at Elpinike, who stood holding by one of its branches the tree where Aristeides had found a seat for himself.

   -That there's a lot more to this than the indictment I can well believe,- said Aristeides.

   Miltiades sat down on the mere stump of an olive tree.

–He's stumped,- Aristeides said, smiling again, before suggesting, to Elpinike: -I'll tell you the gist of what some have been saying, in their political clubs?-

–Yes, do,- she urged him. Her father looked at him, in a certain resigned interest, to hear a familiar theme re-scrutinised.

-This is all secret information,- said Aristeides, confidingly. -But you know how secrets leak out. Sometimes they seem the only things anyone knows much about. The sort of thing I'm about to quote or paraphrase, you might hear from the Alkmaionidai clan, and their associates. Occasionally I'll go a little beyond what they habitually say, into things implied but rarely if ever expressed. Perhaps, Elpinike, after I've spoken their minds, you might tell me if I seem to have a future on the stage - whether I have promise.-

Elpinike looked politely amused and Aristeides began: -'Darius can impose his truth and make it ours. The wealth and even power of the rich may be fairly secure if they support him. If we oppose him, we'll lose everything. We should meekly apologise for burning the city of Sardis. Darius wants to be honoured sincerely. How can he believe our expressions of regret and repentance, if we harbour, protect and listen to this enemy of his? Miltiades' condemnation would be as acceptable to the King as choice offerings brought before him in the palace of Persepolis, by representatives of some subject nation. That much of Miltiades' career is an offence against civilised values, as redefined here, surely we can get the people to see, and reflect in their verdict. To remove him from public life is in the interests of peace and friendship in international relations. With him out of the way, the

Medes and their agents will find it easier to browbeat the rest of our populace and reinstate Hippias as ruler of Athens. It will be like old times, except that our tyrant will be subordinate to Darius, which was not so when Hippias was last in power. We are haunted, not pleasantly, by the thought of Persian dominance, but to accept it is the only way to avoid catastrophe. The former ruler of Athens may make our flesh creep, but there's no practical alternative to saying yes to him and his Persian backers.'-

-Well,- commented Miltiades. -Those Alkmaionids are men of...some sort of glamour, perhaps - and power. Black hearts without principle? Warped characters? Maybe...-

-What have we done to them,- said Elpinike, -to make them behave like this?-

-Anyway,- said Aristeides, -we don't have trial by the Alkmaionidai in Athens. The jury of five hundred can't possibly, as a whole, represent some factional interest.-

-My father too is an actor,- put in Elpinike.

Aristeides looked Miltiades in the eyes to show that his friend was convicted and found guilty of theatrical and not quite convincing despondency.

-I can't celebrate an acquittal that has yet to occur,- Miltiades protested, impatiently, still sitting on his stump. -Who knows how the jury will react? I have more than the Alkmaionidai to fear. I'm comparatively new to Athenian politics - that is, as they are now...-

Chapter 12

I know what's in the back of your mind, father, reflects
Elpinike, and you're right not to mention it. She
catches his eye as he sits near Themistokles, waiting to
be asked to speak, and father and daughter laugh gently
and discreetly, like a gleaming facet of calm rippling
water, across the distance, which to them is no distance
at all. They had not expected to find much to cheer
them up at such a moment.

At last Themistokles signals to Miltiades to begin
speaking; and to one of the clerks to his right to start the
water-clock. Miltiades gets up and moves closer to the
corona, looking from face to face of people who all
have in common that they are not going to determine
the outcome; then turns to face the jury, who seem so
inscrutable. In those quiet moments many can hear the
tranquil splashing of water into the lower jar of the
clock.

-Gentlemen, if you think as badly of me as is
reasonably possible, this trial, however stormy, should
not swirl me into the abyss...-

His energy is in a continuum with that of the corona.
Meanwhile he seems to succeed in not antagonising the
men on whose votes everything depends. Minds are
receptive, interested more in what he may have to say
than in set notions, such as they may have, about him.

Chapter 13

Here Kallidike paused in her reading. She looked down towards the river, where its sinuous flow was modified by some rocks. The Kephisos was not so far away. It traverses the grounds of the estate. She saw a wagtail which alighted, midstream, on one of the rocks. The bird looked around with its customary alertness, eyeing her keenly with the look of truth, the only look it will ever be really interested in, the girl reflected. How far superior in character are animals to human beings, at least in certain ways.

Kallidike said, or rather thought of herself as saying: Just a glance at this handwriting reveals it to me as that of Elpinike. It hasn't really changed since her childhood. It's pleasantly angular and spiky. It's also quite old-fashioned. That kind of *ro,* with two prongs below the loop, is more common in Italy now than in Greece, or so they say. Her contribution here goes beyond the scribal aspects. She worked on the speech at least as much as father did. But they both got help from Aristeides. It was often a matter of my sister and Aristeides working together, before submitting their revisions to the defendant, to include or reject as he saw fit. Almost invariably he would express his approval and accept their modifications and new material. ('This is really just what I meant to say,' was one of his responses. 'Yet I couldn't have said it without your help.') Aristeides remarked to Elpinike, -Oh how we need your authorial voice! To hear it come through - your father being the speaker of words that evolve his own nature, at least to some extent, and everyone else's too - the words of eternal youth - well, at least of someone young enough not to have given up on life - to revive a despondent city, in what has seemed a hopeless situation...-

Kallidike was so often alone that she was used to addressing imaginary audiences. It added to her social experience. Elpinike was rather similar in that respect. But both agreed that it can be less sane than to go all the way by becoming a poet. It was one matter in which to go to extremes was arguably less peculiar than moderation.

-Here then, most dear non-existent audience,- said Kallidike quietly, -is the speech, given to the jury of five hundred, and a widening *corona* of bystanders. It's mostly identical to the text father himself held, to jog his memory. The earliest introductory remarks, which he made sound a bit gauche and were ex tempore, have yet to be added. He was wily enough to realise the value of claiming to be un-practiced as a speaker... But some later off-the-cuff reactions to ploys and tactics of Cleainetos, this version does take account of. As before, Elpinike adds comments and impressions of her own on the trial as she experienced it.-

Kallidike resumed her reading, the text being as follows:

Chapter 14

It is often said that the normal court procedure in which both sides swear to speak the truth is perverse, not to say worse. The two incompatible versions of events cannot both be correct, and someone has to be lying. Cleainetos will have been egged on to credit what he has asserted as prosecutor, and if we put him right he may reply: I wasn't lying for I said what I believed. But this isn't good enough, Cleianetos. Supposing you've been saying what you believed, the lie would still be there. To present as *knowledge* mere suspicion or belief, is to lie. Some say this Cleainetos is an ally of the Alkmaionidai. At any rate it would seem that he has given ear to some rather biased accounts of my life.

You are asked to see me as stained through my associations with the tyranny here in Athens. Surely Hippias and I were hand in glove... That he owed a lot to me, I don't deny. The association of our names conferred on him a false respectability. His closeness to me suggested, for instance, that he was not responsible for my father's death. He used me for a long time to create a misleading aura of innocence. And I'm sure he craved to believe that it was not misleading - that he was as guiltless as he wanted to appear.

Many, noting how much worse his rule got after I had left, have asked themselves was this more than mere coincidence. Contrast the Athens of my partnership with Hippias, and the Athens of increasing violence, of arbitrary arrests and torture, that ensued while I was away. This is some bad influence on my part - untraceable when I'm being closely consulted by the tyrant, but coming into play when I'm far from him, and our mutual alienation is a theme for conversations throughout the Hellenic world and beyond.

I don't want to claim more credit than is my due. Others too of course, Kleisthenes in particular, helped in checking or restraining the excesses of the tyranny. It is enough for my present case that you take into account that no evidence has ever been adduced to link me with the crimes of the regime.

'By tolerating Hippias' rule, Miltiades allowed the oppression to continue.' So you are assured. The suggestion that I could have deposed him had I chosen to do so is flattering, Cleainetos, but also absurd.

Many say that, when you're young, you can put up more easily with the physical discomfort of sinister company. The body then, they say, is more able to endure the effects of oppression and unhappiness. If they are right, I suppose I am fortunate that the tale of my relations with the tyranny is a tale of my youth. Peisistratos died when I was twenty one. My dealings with Hippias overshadowed my twenties and thirties.

He seemed to imply, as he flattered and courted me and my friends, that we should be grateful that he left so many of us alive. But surely, you may say, the *bonhomie* of the palace, in which I shared, wasn't entirely false? Indeed nausea and distaste may be mixed with an unwelcome sweetness. I would come away from there somehow stupefied. One day as I was leaving, a new arrival said to me how charmed he was to see so many children in the palace. Surely, he said,

Hippias is a normal family man, who happens to shoulder great responsibilities for the good of all. I explained to him in a low voice that the children he had seen playing in a nearby room were all hostages, taken from families whom the tyrant deeply distrusted. 'They are here both to deny and to confirm the atmosphere of fear.'

Hipparchos was worth knowing; his milieu of artists, perhaps the best in Greece. When he spoke to you, implying all was well, you might begin to agree. He would have your thoughts fragment, and detach themselves from wider considerations. When he smiled, why shouldn't you smile back? Indeed you might as well. No one denies the contribution he has made to the very fabric of the city. The wall around the Academy, for instance, was built on his instructions. We're not going to have it pulled down because of its association with him. At their best, Hipparchos, and yes, Hippias himself, were or aspired to be true Athenians.

The son of Megakles faced dilemmas similar to mine. A few years into the new reign, Kleisthenes made a reluctant and uneasy archon. 'I'm so pleased to be dishonoured by this honour, or honoured by this dishonour,' he said to me on the day he accepted the magistracy. The following year, I took over from him. We both wanted to get away. Hippias actually felt as uneasy with me as I did with him. He often used to describe time as a healer. Experience showed him the opposite to be true, at least where he and I were concerned. Kleisthenes' belief in equality before the law didn't prevent him from relating to the tyranny in some workaday fashion, without resentment. Please don't leave me…I rely on you, said Hippias to Kleisthenes, as the latter prepared to begin his voluntary exile. With myself and Hippias, it was very different. A poison was there, seeping into our relationship. But the poison would drain away, surely, once I had married his eldest daughter? Of course the human soul has its laws, which don't necessarily comply with our assumptions and theories.

In fact, my marriage to Euphrosyne couldn't improve my interactions with the tyrant. He's bold - I'll grant him that - in the use of his daughters. Some seven years later he would have genuine success with the younger girl, Archedike. Her marriage really would have the effect he desired, of turning old enemies into friends.

My marriage to his elder daughter seemed to emphasise the impossibility of *anything* putting things right between Hippias and myself. He had played his best trick, and it had failed. He grew resigned; he wanted rid of me, and I wanted him to want rid of me. In a grim way I was quite well within, for a change, as I was leaving, despite the difficulties and sombre scenario awaiting me. My life seemed to be starting, bleakly but truly, at the age of thirty-five. As I left Phalerum, both sea and sky were, like my hair, appropriately grey. But at last I was becoming youthful within.

Can it really help my prosecutors to allude to those earlier years, before I was sent to the Chersonese - when Hippias and I were co-operating and sustaining a courteous *modus vivendi*? We were all his obedient subjects then. In the years before I was sent abroad, I was prepared to set aside my personal feelings and help promote the good relations he tended to have with you.

It was good to see the city prosper, partly, as I would like to think, through my own influence. I have sometimes wished I had stayed, and done my best to moderate his rule, and his increasing resentment. But perhaps there was little I could have done. He was never really the same after Hipparchos' death.

Nowadays, everyone talks about how terrible it was in the time of the tyranny. But for the first decade after Peisistratos' death, there was no great opposition to Hippias. For a long time he ruled as responsibly as his father had done. Some were saying at the time, It's as well for a community not to give too much attention to the crimes of its rulers.

Just as Hippias' father Peisistratos was delighted when my uncle and namesake, the son of Kypselos, left to govern the Chersonese, so Hippias himself heaved a sigh of relief when, boarding a trireme, I sailed away, at his command, to our eastern colony. 'You were yourself a tyrant in that place,' they say to me. 'Not in the modern sense,' I reply.

That story about the arrest of the nobles I confess takes me by surprise. I imagined it to be as well understood as it is known. Yes, I arrested them, the reason being their advice to my brother, seven months before his death, to offer the requested symbols of submission to envoys of the Persian King. But the prisoners were released unharmed after a few half-days in custody. The province being, at least in theory, bought and sold, how would you expect me to feel about those *aristoi?* I have faced criticism of the opposite kind, that is, for not taking more serious action against them. It has generally been my way when possible to be mild and easy-going as a ruler and avoid alienating people. But my very mildness has alienated some.

You are aware of my defence of the province against Lampsakos and against some of the contingent tribes. If you know little of the types of legal processes I've been relied on to preside over, and of the verdicts I've given in particular cases, this is I suppose because people were not made to feel cheated or moved to spread accusations against me, of incompetence or unfairness. It is noteworthy that Cleainetos has not been able to rake up a single example of my delivering in court a judgement that came to be generally resented or considered against the interest of the local communities, whether Athenian or barbarian.

Are some of Cleainetos' accusations too absurd for a response? He says I drank wine while on the peninsula. Well I did, yes...and there were some festive occasions to warm the heart of Aphrodite. So what? Things he adduces as accusations, elicit the approval of the wise - certainly not their censure.

Both love and wine have helped improve my relations with my subjects. Love is best, really, that's where you find Dionysos at his truest. Wine is a more uncertain guide to him. Lust and possibly for some people drink (in moderation) are handmaids of good judgment and sanity in personal relations and the governance of nations. The other gods accept Dionysos and Aphrodite, and those two are quite at home with Athena and Hephaestus. Meanwhile Justice, one of the oldest of the gods, is always looking for an opportunity to return to the earth. No one by theorising or some act of will tears away several of the colours of the rainbow, and Cleainetos' impugning my own right and that of others on the peninsula to their full range of concerns and activities - well it seems bizarre to me. But what do you think?

(Smiles and quiet laughter from many, at this point.)

Persian envoys visiting my court were always polite and if manners were anything to go by, you wouldn't suppose they intended any harm. Of course they were pleased with the province - that soon before my arrival it had made a promise, to go back on which would be considered out of the question. For a while we didn't have to do much to avoid Persian violence and indignation. Some began to reflect: It's an easy thing to be a friend of Persia. There is nothing strange or unnatural about it. It isn't a problem after all. But when the King decided now was the time to bring you into his empire as a subject, you knew what threats you would face if you refused. Ahura Mazda and the other gods have witnessed your promise! You must stand by it! How immoral it would be, to behave as free men! Don't even imagine yourselves free.

I had been in the Chersonese a few years when for the first time the Medes entered Europe in considerable force. I myself and other leaders in western Asia and the isles were ordered to co-operate with the imperial invasion, which at first was directed primarily against Scythia. You are aware that I obeyed my instructions - that I sailed the Black Sea and along the Ister, to remain at the bridge of boats, and await the King's return from his campaign. Some of you may have heard suggestions that the story of my attempt to break the bridge was made up to enhance my prestige here in Athens. Miltiades says he incurred the King's displeasure! He dared do no such thing! - it is sometimes claimed, or insinuated. But if you were to assume me not to have endangered a Persian army and its ability to return over that wide river, a number of later events would become less easy to explain. Why did I escape from the Chersonese a few decades ago, once it became clear that the Medes meant to consolidate and extend their power in Europe? Why would I have anything to fear from them? I was *already* as much in danger *then*, as I was last month, during the Phoenician pursuit of my ships as I was on my way to this place. Many here who through seafaring and trade come into contact with the Medes and their allies will confirm how I behaved at the Ister. It's not something the barbarians are prone to forget, that a campaign already very fraught with troubles could have been catastrophic had my colleagues not vetoed my proposal that we break up the bridge and leave the King and his army trapped in enemy territory.

I have effectively been exiled three times, twice from the peninsula, once from here. In all three cases it was for the same reasons: my opposition to despotic authority, and its hostility towards me.

Cleainetos' assertion that when I left the Chersonese nineteen years back I did so to escape from the Scythians, is strange considering how well I got on with those admittedly rather savage gentlemen. I left the place accompanied by quite a number of them, my comrades and supporters. Our friendship was by then of some months' standing. We had been as one in wishing to destroy the bridge over the Ister. Perhaps my alienation from my Ionian colleagues enhanced my comradeship with the Scythian wild men, who were perfectly trustworthy. We rode south together. Those who entered the Chersonese, I accompanied. But soon afterwards we were informed that the Persian army intended to make its way to the coast via the peninsula itself. Neither I nor my Scythians would have been at all wise to try and coexist on a narrow stretch of land with the wounded lion of Persia. As the huge army approaches, I am supposedly to take fright, not at it, but at my northern friends! That we were scared of Darius' army, no one here will find difficult to believe. There is nothing discreditable in my escaping, for the power I faced was one that I had no means of opposing with any hopes of success. Had Darius caught me I would have been tortured and killed.

During my exile from the Chersonese I wrote off my marriage to Hippias' daughter, who after all was so distant, and we were not communicating with each other... I took a new wife, the eldest daughter of the Thracian King Olorus, with whom I was staying. She died in childbirth. Some fourteen months later I would marry her younger sister, Hegesipyle. She was the sole surviving offspring of Olorus and I didn't want to deprive him of her company. For nine years she and I were living as part of the royal household. My impressions and experience of the locality were augmented by very little information indeed about what was going on here. But some obscure news of revolution and social change did eventually get through to me. Some of the messengers thought I should feel alarmed and advised me against ever returning.

Soon after Olorus' death I took my decision to reveal my trust in you. I sailed home with my family... The atmosphere here in those days, is pleasant for me to recall. My daughters were of an age to take part in the rites of Artemis at Brauron, and they felt as Athenian as anyone as they joined other girls in her service. It was an Athens after my own heart, to which I returned.

Behind the only cloud, or attempted cloud, over my return, was a certain Lysagoras of Paros, a former associate of mine. During an audience at Halicarnassus with Darius' old friend Hydarnes, Lysagoras assured him of the goodwill of his home island towards Persia, and asked for money. Having discussed the latest gossip, he reminded Hydarnes of the peril a Persian army had been in ten years earlier through my machinations; assured him that my opinions and aspirations were the same as ever; that I was back in Athens; and that if he, Hydarnes, knew what was good for him, and for his fellow Persians, he would urge the Athenians to reject me - that is, refuse to let me dwell on my estate, or indeed anywhere in their territory. Having commended Lysagoras for his zeal and the loyalty of Paros, Hydarnes sent an ambassador to address the council here, and warn what their accepting me would seem to imply. The council responded that as an Athenian citizen I had the right to live here; that their policies were their own and not controlled by Persia; but that on the other hand, this being a democracy, there was no inevitable agreement between my opinions and politics, and those of my fellow citizens. The ambassador returned to Caria, mission unaccomplished, and Hydarnes let the matter drop.

Four years into my stay at Athens, the issue of the Ionian revolt came for the first time before the council and assembly. They learnt that tens of thousands of Ionians were at one in opposition to Darius and that, of the tyrants of the region, some had abdicated, others been deposed. Aristagoras of Miletos had stepped down, but was soon afterwards elected general. Koes of Lesbos, who had received the tyranny of that isle for his especial loyalty at the Ister, was stoned to death. For most of the old tyrants, it was a matter of accepting a new life of obscurity in a sort of tremulous gratitude that their lives and to some extent possessions had been spared.

Once I had got a fairly clear view, from various reports, of the state of things on the peninsula (from which the Persian administrators, alarmed by news of insurrection to the south, had fled) I decided to return. It was said that Persian forces along the Thracian coast and in northern Greece, were overstretched; that it was as much as they could do to maintain their garrisons, and that they were in no position to reassert the King's authority in the Chersonese. I arrived in the colony to see if I could make myself useful, and, as before, was welcomed as governor. I don't recall anyone there casting doubt on the legality of my rule.

Here in Greece, Aristagoras of Miletos was travelling from place to place, begging for support. Uncertain how to react, the Argives consulted Delphic Apollo. His oracle, generous in information, predicted disaster for both cities - for Argos herself, and for Miletos. The Argives stayed aloof. Sparta did likewise - preferring to fulfil the first half of the prophecy by inflicting calamity upon Argos, than to dwell on the crisis abroad. Aristagoras, leaving the Peloponnese, came to Athens. Would the people here help him? At last he got the response he had craved. Eretria too consented to help.

Your relations with Persia were deteriorating, before
this. Six years earlier, Artaphernes had told your
ambassadors to Sardis, 'the Athenians must take
Hippias back, if they want to be safe.' Your refusal to
comply put you in a state almost of undeclared war with
Persia. But Darius was a busy man and Athens of no
great importance in his eyes. If you now have his deep
hatred, it's because of your support for the Ionian
rebellion, and role, some six years ago, in the
destruction of his western capital. The revolt as it
developed both supplied the incentive for war against us
and rendered it for the time being impractical. In the
course of the revolution, even the Chersonese, so much
closer to the conflict, passed a number of tranquil years.
It's an uneasy peace - that which is the gift of a war
which you know to be increasingly bloody, and not so
far away.

It was something, wouldn't you say, to have
Athenians in control on the peninsula? Better than the
scenario lately re-imposed, of rule by Persia. Like other
Ionian generals and leaders, I sought to promote and
confirm the independence of the whole region. At the
Pan-Ionian conference I pledged my financial support
for the revolution. In the event I supplied more money
than several of the rebel cities put together. They had
been taxed heavily by Darius in the era prior to the
revolt, and unlike me had no ready access to much
silver.

During this period, the Aegean was ours; the
imperial navy wary of sailing it. Conditions being
favourable, I set to work establishing the Athenian
colonies on Imbros and Lemnos. It has been said that I
expelled the entire Pelasgian population of the latter

isle. In fact those natives who acquiesced in the colonial plan were allowed to remain. But, yes, those who opposed it were ejected.

In the following few years I was often absent from the peninsula. My son Metiochos was used to standing in for me as governor. During my time in Asia I was able to observe for myself the terrifying success of some Persian armies in action. A domestic issue also kept me away: the return of my daughters, whom I accompanied here to Athens. I remained with them for a few months, busying myself (directly for a change, rather than through bailiffs) with my estate - the patriotic duty, of course, of every Athenian who wants to produce a surplus and have money enough to help supply the needs of the city. About a year ago I was once more on Lemnos, where I introduced my thirteen year old son Kimon to the local population, and them to him; and sorted out some judicial and administrative problems that had arisen in my absence.

On my return from Lemnos I learned of the presence at Byzantium of the wily Histiaios, former governor of Miletos.

For a long era - indeed from within a year of our being together as colleagues at the Ister - he had been in a sort of captivity at Susa. He was Darius' special advisor, supposedly; but it was understood that he was not allowed to leave. The King had been tremendously grateful to him for his standing by a badly frightened Persian army and getting it safely across the river; had rewarded him with further wealth and power, and command of a city on the edge of the new dominions within Europe; only to be warned by his friend, the general Megabazos - yes, early on, some eighteen years ago, it will be - not to give free reign to this Greek. Megabazos complained to the King at Sardis that to consider Histiaios is like seeing treble. 'He's building up your power...his own, and both at once. His spirit is un-Persian and would I believe in the long run stir up our calm sea of subjection. Be careful, or one day there'll be a storm of his making. He is driven by impulses which belie his words of loyalty to you, however sincere they may be.' It was on Megabazos' advice, that Darius summoned Histiaios to Susa. There the Greek experienced the luxuries of barbarian munificence. He had everything, as Darius would say. For sixteen years he languished, for the four latest of them trying to get on well with the former tyrant of this place. (Hippias had long preferred the Troad and Hellespontine region as his place of exile, ignoring Darius' offers of hospitality. But the need to escape the Ionian revolutionaries induced Hippias to change his mind and journey to Susa.) Histiaios pined for the Aegean. 'Hestia, goddess of the hearth...' he would be heard to say, while reflecting on the significance of his own name, which seemed to confirm his inability to accept being away from places he could identify as home. He finally persuaded Darius to let him go, on the understanding that he work to end the revolt. Darius was still grateful for his good service at the Ister, and that the Milesian was himself among the original instigators of the rebellion, the King had not yet come to believe or even suspect.

At Byzantium Histiaios commanded a number of ships, which he had brought from Lesbos. He joined his forces with those of the locality to afford much needed protection to Hellenic trade through the Bosporus. My own ships, patrolling the sea further west, were the safer and more effective for his help. Even in the later months of the revolt, our power significantly curtailed the predatory reach of the Persian navy. Far from trying to end the rebellion, Histiaios was a faithful co-worker in the Hellenic cause. When he learnt of the defeat of the Ionian fleet near the island of Lade, he left Byzantium with his followers. On his way...he wasn't quite sure where, he visited me at Sestos, where he urged me to set sail for Athens as soon as possible. 'The last major stronghold of resistance, Miletos, is under siege,' he said, as if that decided the matter. I replied: 'I'm aware of this. But by the time the city falls, it will be winter, and the season will keep things militarily quiet for some months.'

I reminded him how vehement an opponent of mine he had been a few decades back, at the Ister conference. He gave a wan smile and said, 'We could have had an Ionian revolt so long ago. What have I done with my life? - helped start a revolt that's being crushed; and vetoed one that would have stood a better chance of success.' It's five months now, since that reunion. Apparently, early last month, he and his men were attacked on the mainland opposite Lesbos by a Persian army under the general Harpagos. Most of Histiaios' men were killed. He himself was captured, brought to Sardis, and there impaled on the instructions of Artaphernes, who had long despised Darius' indulgence of the wandering Greek.

In midwinter I was joined at Eion by the historian Hekataios. In the dark evenings we would discuss how the revolt might be renewed. With the approach of spring, we were forced to accept that Ionian resistance as a large-scale force was extinct. Yet my hopes for the Chersonese and for islands whose eastern cliffs have so often been felt to face Asia in a spirit of defiance, remained. I imagined many refugees might gather on the peninsula and make it very difficult for the Mede to get a foothold there. But in fact, not over-blessed with reinforcements, we faced the prospect of feeling, and indeed being, increasingly weak and isolated.

On learning that the Phoenicians had reached Tenedos, I travelled with my followers and sons to the farther side of the peninsula, where a non-militarised sea seemed to await us. We manned five ships, piling into them what money and valuables we could salvage. Setting sail into the Black Gulf, we hoped we were far enough north to escape easily. But the Phoenician fleet, sighting us, gave chase. The ship commanded by my son Metiochos was captured. Whether he is alive or dead, I don't know, but it's clear I'll never see him again. I put in at Imbros with my remaining four ships, and the Phoenicians sailed off with their prize. The local populace re-expressed gratitude for my founding their colony and remarked, more kindly than accurately: 'This is your island.' Their hospitality was some consolation, even to me, as we discussed with them the six years of revolt. The next day I set sail for Athens.

For over a month now, I've been once more among you. Are you as dangerous and hostile to me as the Phoenicians and their Persian masters? Should I have tried to make my escape from here, rather than stand trial? Well…I have been your servant for so long, not democratically indeed, as I should have been, but militarily and as a leader of men, that it wouldn't feel right for me to seek a destiny elsewhere. I live and die an Athenian.

According to Cleainetos, I should receive no welcome or acceptance in a democracy. Yet I was here for some years, prior to the Ionian revolt, and no one prosecuted me. Better late than never, Cleainetos is saying. If, as he desires, I now lose everything, you will never know whether I could have made myself useful in the coming conflict. You hold my fate in your hands. Do you feel that the law was ever meant to hurt the sort of ruler I have been? My family as you know have traditionally represented Spartan interests. Visitors from Lakedaimon receive from us appropriate honour, according to the will of Zeus Xenios. Perhaps the fact that I wasn't in town when you so bravely expelled Cleomenes and his entourage might stand me in good stead as I try to be a bridge between you and your new allies.

As long as I can I will give you the advice I feel it is my duty to impart. Not least among this is that, to have a chance to sustain our independence, we will have to stop attacking each other. I recommend we set aside the thought of many a past crime and enmity, as we prepare to meet the coming onslaught. Far from depriving loyal citizens of their rights, you should be asking who else should be enfranchised. There are slaves here who should be freed. - They would fight for you, if you would let them. Within this month, I may be elected general of my tribe. Or I may be an outcast, with no rights, not even that to life itself. If you trust me, I believe I can show why you were right to do so. This is not just a matter of the fate of a private individual. To that extent, Cleainetos is right. Don't maim the State and its powers by refusing my help. I'm not some outside agency, some alien. I am as Athenian as Solon, as anyone. I am one of you. To attack me would be to inflict injury upon yourselves. If you acquit me I shall do all I can with the help of the gods to defend you and all that you stand for and believe in.

Chapter 15

The momentary silence at the close of the speech is followed by a burst of applause from the *corona*. –A musical pause,- Elpinike says, without hearing her own voice. Miltiades takes her hand as he comes to sit by her. Soon even the jury are judiciously clapping. Then the quietness seems expectant. –The water is still flowing,- one of the jurors points out. Miltiades laughs, as do many others, and there is an almost festive sense to the occasion as he looks around to receive many glances of people welcoming him to that moment of their experience. He rises once more to append some remarks on the *nous* of the populace, whose behaviour, he says, -will forever put to shame the lesser men who rage and rant through their lives and blight those of others for an empty, a specious glory. I am happier to be of the Athenian *demos* than I could ever be to rule over others.-

As the jurors are filing past the jar in which they will cast their votes - the hollow or the solid bronze, as the case may be - he looks questioningly at Themistokles, who nods as if the opportunity he seeks is still there for the taking. Miltiades glances round, and adds:

-Some of you may want to forget international events and the coercive power of Darius, and think merely of personal and domestic concerns. But certain things should be kept in mind. It's dangerous to say, we can go back, when you've already moved on to a more developed state of mind. You are not adornments to someone else's triumph. Under a despot, frustration would be a sickness, an inhuman thing, offensive to you, of no use to anyone - except one man, I suppose.

-No, you can't go back. Barbarians are obsessed with getting their fellow men to submit. 'We have, so why shouldn't others?' they think. They're constantly looking over their shoulders asking themselves, do I win approval with this observation? Among them, life can never be sufficiently *écrasée.*

-The slaves receive more honour here, than the mass of Darius' subjects generally do. Forever puerile, are the willing slaves of the King. Don't trust, don't believe in his world. It's not moving on. It never will. Don't let him make life stale and old where even the elderly are youthful in spirit. You can't afford to dare to lack courage...-

The *corona* begins to cheer once more. Some exclaim, -Son of Kimon!- while others, perhaps considering this rather prosaic, prefer the cry: -Son of Ajax!- Apparently even in a democracy, kinship with high class characters depicted in the *Iliad* is not to be despised or undervalued.

Elpinike comes to join her father, who is in conversation with the judge. As those two are still absorbed in mutual thought and an exchange of views, a clerk, a document in his hand, approaches. He waits patiently for the judge to notice him, and call or make some signal for silence. In the meantime he remarks, smiling, to Elpinike: -This confirms the impression...-

She glances at the papyrus. Her father has four hundred and sixty five votes in his favour…

Chapter 16

Kallidike wound the end of the papyrus round the rest of the coil and, moving carefully at first, eventually jumped from the olive tree. Among the young grasses, a snake was looking up at her. How quiet and harmonious is this brutal world... I'll go in for a herbal infusion...

On entering the men's room, which seemed void of occupants, she heard a deeply-felt growl. She turned and noted in the shady room, that her father's amiable dog had promoted himself to one of the couches. That big and powerful mastiff, who was free from all perplexities about his own or anyone's future, would growl at her on sight each day. It had been his custom, ever since she had intruded on his territory by moving into the country. Elpinike, yes, he would growl at her too. –I've had enough of you,- said Kallidike, hurrying on.

To her aunt Alexandra, whom she saw in the kitchen, she said she felt hungry; and anxious about the marriage question.

That Alexandra was quite old you could infer from her face, but her movements seemed easily made and without impediments. She was slim and lively, and her spirit would sometimes incline people to say to themselves: She must know or have a good idea what the universe is like, so how can she be so cheerful?

-Here comes Barbaros,- she said.

-Ah, Barbaros!- said Kallidike sceptically, as the dog she had seen in the men's room quietly approached to rest his head in her lap in peace, trust and goodwill. Indeed his expression looked suspiciously like one of love and adoration. This was by no means the first time he had behaved like this towards her, quite soon after growling and succeeding (at least to some extent) in scaring her. There seemed to be no concept at all, no inkling in that doggy brain, of logical and rational consistency.

-You're as shameless in affection as in growls,- said the girl.

-Get yourself some of the cold barley broth,- said Alexandra, who had begun to slurp some herself. -It's a poor stomach that can't warm its own food. I can also offer you cold comfort.-

-I'll warm that up too,- said Kallidike, getting up from the chair she had settled on, to go over to the oven, on which a bowl of the said broth had been placed to keep warm. —Yes, it's as cold as the oven - and the room,- she confirmed. She ladled the food into a smaller bowl for herself, chose one of the silver spoons dangling from the wall (the spoon she chose was familiar to her from her Thracian childhood), and returned to the table. Barbaros, who had been waiting for this moment, rested his head again in her warm lap, and looked up at her with those eyes of calm trust and good nature.

-Ah…the marriage question,- said Alexandra from the opposite side of the table. As she sat there, she leaned on it with one elbow and looked from behind her bedraggled hair. The way she let it dangle seemed to suggest some sort of shield and a distancing herself from things others went in for and accepted. -You know my approach. I'm a Hestia, an old maid. I'm good at reassuring others in matters where I was never able to reassure myself.- She paused, and seemed to find it quite interesting to empathise with the poor girl in front of her. -Husbands and wives...they never speak to each other, you know. It'll be fine. He'll just ignore you.-

-You're sure? You're not having me on?- said Kallidike, grating some cheese over her broth.

-Anyway,- said Alexandra, -you'll have a new alternative home, to add to the others.-

-It's a pleasant house, near the sea.- Kallidike sighed.

-You sigh like the sea herself,- said Alexandra.

-I thought it might improve my mood, to hear my own words.-

-You'll spend most of your time with the women.-

-But I might have to bear a child,- said Kallidike, putting aside the cheese-grater, with its handle in the shape of a crouching, ready-to-pounce lion. She glanced jadedly at the design, which comic poetry, for instance, tended to allude to as suggestive of someone preparing to have sex.

-If you do conceive, you'll experience an amazing joy that will remain with you over the following months.-

-Women with child have spoken to you of this?-

-They have, but I was aware of it anyway. To be with them is to sense the joy they receive from the gods; often to share in it. If you find yourself having to give birth...well, try and accept being in the hands of Artemis, Apollo's virgin sister.-

-I was almost looking forward to marriage while it seemed to approach in the guise of a dream,- confessed Kallidike. -The reality scares me. To be pleased with it - well - wouldn't it be like being pleased with a death sentence?-

-Life's a death sentence, marriage a possible one,- said Alexandra. -Most women survive. Look how many widows there are, still young, of men killed in battle. Some at least can't wait to get re-married.-

-My own and Kimon's mother, Hegesipyle, died in childbirth; so too did Elpinike's mother.-

-Women giving birth scream in anguish,- conceded Alexandra.

-I don't mind pain as long as it doesn't hurt.-

-You don't crave - the divine thing?-

-We use dildos - myself and Elpinike - like most women. We give ourselves orgasms - which by the way seem somehow to stimulate a certain interest in the cat. I don't think either of us - I mean, either me or my sister, really feel a need for sexual intercourse. How many women *pretend* to need it - to reassure their men? 'Oh darling I'm longing for it, and you...'-

-Often they're not,- Alexandra admitted. -Or so they tell me. It can seem better to deceive than induce sulks and ill temper... You could back out, say no to the marriage if you wished.-

-Oh, I'll probably go through with it. My impression of my man to be is that he won't hurt me any more than it's normal for human beings to hurt each other. He won't attack me physically or shout at me. There's something feminine about him that I like. Anyway, as you were saying (at least, I think it's what you *meant*), he'll probably ignore me much of the time.-

After a few moments' pause, she added: -Elpinike seems more in trouble than we realised.-

-I know,- said Alexandra, -in part because of the scandal involving her, many are speaking of Kimon as a likely candidate for ostracism.-

-I've so often heard Elpinike use the term metaphorically... But yes, it seems Kimon could be exiled, should he try for political eminence.-

-They'll *want* to banish not only him but Elpinike also.- Alexandra added: -I say to Kimon: from the start of your career, be generous. Produce plays about down–and-outs and you won't become one yourself. Finance more liturgies than the State demands of you. 'But it doesn't look as though I'll have the money,' he says to me. 'You are surely aware of this. Our family is increasingly impoverished. Of course we might sell land. But we would be eroding the basis of our claim to a high social status.'-

-They can't strictly speaking ostracise Elpinike,- said Kallidike. -I suppose it would be flattering in a way to do that - make an exception for her, thus ascribing to her great political power. But of course she lacks it, as all women do. Ostracism in its literal sense is a special honour, reserved only for men.-

-For men eminent on the political and military stage - yes, of course. But Kimon's exile, should it occur, could affect Elpinike quite seriously, along with the rest of us. She might choose to go into exile with him.-

Kallidike pulled a sceptical face. -It's premature really, to allude to a career which has yet to begin. When he's eighteen in four years from now, and subsequently, he may not even attempt leadership. He seems to lack ambition.-

There was a pause. Kallidike began to stroke the head of Barbaros. As always when she did that, he withdrew from her hand. He seemed unable to accept even a careful and gentle touch to his forehead. He hurried off.

-We're all shaken by the loss of Metiochos,- said Alexandra. —He and our long-term ambitions seemed somehow synonymous. More than any of us, he seemed to be the one with a significant destiny. Kimon…well…he doesn't seem to take himself seriously.-

Alexandra added: -I know that Elpinike has been doing some writing, in prose as well as verse. If you can't be central to historical events I suppose you have all the more leisure, if you wish, to write about them. She is an exile from her birth - like all women - because of her gender.-

-Men are in exile from us, and we from them,- suggested Kallidike, -and this is so even when we're most intimate.-

The Capture of Miletos

Preface

A drama on the capture of Miletos, by Phrynichos son of Polyphrasmon, was produced (perhaps by Themistokles) in the theatre of Dionysos, in early spring 493 BCE.

'The theatre burst into tears...' and the poet was fined heavily for reminding the people of events that had already distressed them greatly.

Their Iliadic readiness to express emotion, one is wary of over-interpreting. Within a few years these Athenians will be defeating the barbarian army at Marathon.

Phrynichos' play represents a stage in the psychological development, and genesis of a city that will be a paradigm, political and cultural, for future generations, and perhaps indeed (in accordance with the prophecy), 'an eagle in the clouds forever'.

The present text is an attempt to resuscitate the most controversial of Phrynichos' plays.

Dramatis Personae

Chorus of women of Miletos
Datis, a Persian general
Artaphernes, nephew of the Persian King
Ghost of Evalkidas, a Greek general
Apollo, son of Zeus
Guards and soldiers of the Persian army

Notes:

The Satrap Artaphernes, governor of Sardis, is the
father of the above character of the same name.
The first syllable of the name Datis sounds rather like
the English word 'dart', the alpha being long.

The scene is a sandy beach in a bay, close to Miletos.
To the right, before a defensive wall, is a siege tower.
The wall is broken and jagged, fallen masonry being
strewn nearby. At the centre it is not much higher than
ground level, from which a series of uneven and
accidental 'steps' lead up to the unimpaired far left
surface. Through the gap in the wall damaged houses
are visible. In the far distance, a large building is in
flames.

Time: midwinter, a few months before the
production of the play.

Enter: Chorus of Milesian women with a number of
children. The latter sit down on rocks, fallen bits of
masonry, or the lower floor of the siege engine. Persian
guards accompany them.

Chorus Leader (an older, matronly figure):
   Let's move beyond the shadow of the walls,
Kore (a girl of about fifteen):
   Those walls that we once helped to man.
Chorus leader: Our guards
   Won't mind - will you? - for you'll be warmer
      too.
   Our feet don't sink into the sand. How fierce
   Our captors are when we suggest to them
   What might be done!
Kore: They think that we should fawn.
   'You'll lose your nature,' they all seem to say,
   'Both pride and self-assurance.'
Chorus leader: Time, if we live, will tell.

Chorus: We view the sea and coast,
And hope our memories
Of these and of our homes
Will never fade in exile.
The waves are tarnished bronze. An icy breeze
Blows from them. To keep warm we move.

Still, as we dance upon this shore
We wring our hands, remembering
The flow, this Artemisian month
Of refugees from lost battles,
Seeking safety within our walls;
Safety! - the inevitable storm
Of Persian arms within the gates,
Advancing so remorselessly…

Kore: At first as all that panoply
Of alien arms approached the walls -
That it was there to put paid to
Our lives and kill the day for us,
Extinguishing its light,
Was more than I could understand -
Until of course I saw the people dying.
I wasn't used to being under threat,
You see; my parents never threatened me.

Chorus: That army is so colourful -
The gaudy pageant of the Medes -
Their ensigns and their battle dress.
The intricate scaly armour…its
Multiple sheen has dazzled our
Bewildered minds as if it were

Some emblem of superiority
(Which I suppose it is, in part)…

Those siege towers are a wonder - so well made
And monumental…as protective to
Their riders as fatal to us.
You see, they are safe in waging war,
Those brave barbarians.

Kore: Some Persian words and exclamations
Resound in my mind's ear. *Arta -*
What does it mean?
Chorus: *Arta?* Justice.
Kore: Spara, aspa?
Chorus: A shield, a horse.
Kore: Ahura Mazda, their good god,
Was often on their lips, of course.
Chorus: Some people on our own side we have killed,
Their wounds being so terrible. Their cries
Are heavy iron chains that chafe.
They're drawn within and dragged over our hearts.
When we're asleep they draw us towards Hades.
Leader: But none of us, despite our wish,
Has seemed to cross the river Styx.
Kore: I dreamed I offered myrtle, rosemary,
And mint to Charon; but he smirked at these,
Trampling them underfoot inside his boat,
And waving me away. Then when I sang
Some songs of Sappho and Anacreon
He sneered and said, 'Who do you think you are?
Sweet Orpheus?' Meanwhile great multitudes
Of dead men climbed aboard his boat.
Then Charon said to me, 'Not yet!

I won't yet ferry you towards
The other side to meet your love
In groves of white and yellow asphodel.'
Chorus: Our past has much in it to inform
Us of our prospects...who we are...
Our bodies and their dregs of souls
Now make a mockery, perhaps,
Of what we knew before.
All is belied and falsified
And violently cast aside.
We're dislocated from ourselves.
Our lives are in the dead city...
Chorus leader: Don't pause, or do you want to hear
Our captors as they celebrate
And boast of their destructive might?
Chorus: I see emerging from the gates
Datis the Mede, commander of
The fleet, which in last moon's dotage
Defeated ours.
Kore: Beside him is a younger man,
Proud Artaphernes, son of Artaphernes.
What finery he wears, of golden anklets
And bracelets...
Chorus leader: ...gaudy trousers...
Kore: I noticed them as well. ...Blue, saffron, red.
That purple cloak alone insinuates
That even Datis should look up to him,
The nephew of Darius, King of kings.
Chorus leader: They leer at us, now walk in our
direction.
You'd think they both were mariners
Who hadn't found their land-legs yet.
There's deep excitement in their vivid eyes.

What shall we say? Would flattery appease?

(Enter Datis and Artaphernes.)

Brave Datis, victor on the salty sea,
And Artaphernes, co-victor with him
In seas of wine and blood, would you accept
  The praise of those whose lives you have brought
  low?
Datis (to the captives): As long as you don't think
    Your words could be of value in our eyes.
    We come to see that all is as it should be -
    No prisoners escaped, nor guards gone off
    To satiate themselves within the town.
Artaphernes: It may be as well to avert our eyes from
      several
      Of these women. Threnodic melodies
      Go well with looks like theirs. Their living death
      They seem to feel could dart destructively
      To us from their fierce eyes.
Datis: Survivors of Miletos, if you'd take
    A larger view, you would reform your glances
    And give up your threnodic, dirge-like songs.
    To build a better world much sacrifice
    Will always be required, it's in the nature
    Of things, the gods decree it must be so.
    Through our great King of kings all nations must
    Become one, learn to live in peace and quiet.
Artaphernes: Admit you knew you couldn't win -
      accept
      The destiny Apollo has foretold.
Datis: What wretches - having lost their former lives
      Forever, they believe they can say no

To things as they are now!
> *To the women:*

You say you love
Freedom, that mirage of the unhinged soul.
Our many spies, including the King's Eye
(So called) and Ears have searched out your
  beliefs,
Your aberrations of the intellect.
Without freedom, you say, your lives would be
Asphyxiated... All your nonsense forms
An interesting dossier for our King.

Chorus: Our freedom...

Datis: ...has betrayed you, led you to
Deep misery and ruin. - Cease your faith.
Don't value a delusion.

Artaphernes: Once it was
Open to you to live that lie, that cause
Of endless woes; not now. Truth presses on you.

Datis: How foolish you all are! Your independence
Has been a boon indeed, but not to you!

Artaphernes: Your lone hero is easiest to degrade,
A few cities alone against the world
So easily defeated and enslaved.

Datis: Look south now, at those flames...

Chorus: That they are from
Apollo's temple - yes, of course, we know.

Artaphernes: When holy things of yours have been
  despoiled
And desecrated, then the truth sinks home,
You feel defeated in your deepest soul.

Chorus: Apollo will avenge your sacrilege.
Before your military triumphs there's
Another - of hubristic fantasy.

Datis: Not so, not so, we don't offend the gods
    With high thoughts of ourselves, for we believe
    Less in ourselves as born to rule, than in
    Yourselves as made for scorn and grinding under
    Our military boots.
Artaphernes: In this world all
    Will be degraded - some indeed
    Will be more so than others. It's the rule
    Reflecting royal wisdom
    Whose deep, rich mysteries
    Play in Darius' smile.
    You see we are philosophers as well
    As being the greatest generals in our army.
Chorus: We should have got enlightened years ago.
    Why didn't we? We should have learnt from you.
Datis: We are taught to ride, shoot with the bow, and
      speak
    Plain truths. Now under our improving power
    You are more honest than you mean to be.
    Your irony won't take; and even you
    Can see you are no longer subtle snakes.
Artaphernes: Your range and scope of thought must
      atrophy.
    Your good volcano is the sort that's capped.
    There is in your Greek lands a very bad one,
    Or so they say - disgrace of a volcano -
    Which stays active - mount Aetna, is that it?
    Such is the Hellenic mind - in flux and restless
    Where it most needs something to hold it still,
    Some power that saves it from the kind of thoughts
    That erodes faith in our authority.
    The mind that can think independently
    Presents a danger to our despotism.

To cap the mind, pour over it the glue
Of approved attitudes, that is our mission.
Oh ladies, would you think your way to freedom?
Accept being bored with things and with
    yourselves.
Datis: You'll be the more secure when you're
    persuaded
You're incapable of thoughts worth mentioning
Apart from those we give you.
You should be self-destroying for your good,
Eclipsing the old mount Aetna of your souls,
Quite lowly but no less so than your men -
Those who survive - the eunuchs of our power
Subservient to us in every way.
We need more women in the town. - Guards,
    bring
Another twelve, the fairest ones, of course.
Those others that we took before, bring back.

Datis steps forward to address the audience.

You Greeks are inconsistent - you have slaves.
We merely say that all should be as they are.
The era of enlightened slavery
Is now at hand. Its causes are within you.
You'll find in your own souls reasons enough
To be the humble servants of our King.

Exeunt Datis and Artaphernes.

The chorus leader seems to address not only Athenians
but guests from other cities, as she sings:

But you who truly live,
Know joy in furthering your needs,
Was there not more - there *was* - you could have
    done
To save our cities,
The Hellas of the East - Ionia.
Tragic success, raising false hopes, was all
You won for us, Athenians!
- Who have encouraged us in our revolt,
Sending a force of twenty ships to help us,
Which then withdrew and left us to our fate.

After a pause the whole chorus sings sardonically:

How hard *they* work - the servants of the King -
To keep themselves and others in subjection!
How their authority
Now laps as sludge against the crystalline
Clear spirit that we thought was ours, not theirs.

They do acknowledge our humanity
In their own way. To them humanity
Implies a laughable susceptibility
To pleasure, pain and terror. Man exists
To be manipulated and despised.

The commentary of the double pipes often harmonises
with the tune of the chorus. But sometimes a triple
discord arises, to which one might ascribe a variety of

*meanings - the soul trying to escape from itself; from
the body, from sanity...*

*Enter: a man whose mask is bloody and death-pale.
His ghostly nature is easily inferred. It's not just the
face; his steady walk seems that of one whom nothing
physical impedes.*

*At his approach the chorus stand quite still. He will
speak in a deep, occasionally tremulous voice,
suggesting an uneasy, reluctant and dismayed
association with the depths of Earth. He is not seen or
heard by the guards.*

Ghost (to the Chorus):
    The realm of young Persephone repels
    You too, it seems, though in a different sense.
    I can't accept my death, nor you your life.
    We come together in your waking dream.
    Our meeting is in No Place.
Chorus: We have thought
    A ghost would make us tremble, shrink away,
    But as it is we're almost reassured.
    Clearly, you are no healthy persecutor.
    Are you a casualty of our war?
    What city are you from?
Ghost: Eretria.
    The five ships sent to Ephesus from there
    To help the revolution, I commanded.
    You may have heard my name - Evalkidas.
Chorus: You are - or were - they say, a great athlete.
Evalkidas: Simonidean songs praise my prowess
    In running and (three times) as charioteer.

The First guard puts aside stylus and tablet and

approaches the women.

First Guard: You're in some conversation?
Second guard (also stepping forward):
                              Leave them be.
First guard (to the women):
    Your visitant's an apparition, merely.
    You understand?
            (to his comrades):
                    It seems they've synthesised
    Their madness.
Chorus leader: True, we share the same
        delusion.
Second guard (to the women):
    Calamity has thrown your frame of mind
    To where some spirits keep you company.
    Is that the case?
            (To the first guard):
                    However that may be
    Let's stand or sit apart. If you inhibit
    Their speech and interfere like this,
    Then that report of yours to King Darius
    Will I suspect be of less value than
    It should have been. To slaves one should allow
    A little freedom. Then you'll know what they
    Are really like, and how best to control them.

*The first guard seems to delay his withdrawal, as if
interfering with the chorus is of more interest to him.
He is both intrigued by them and in a mind to mock
them. He looks into the eyes of some as if to call in
question their right to experience things as they do. The
second and third guard draw him away impatiently.*

Second guard: These women may enjoy such gifts of
    soul
    As needs must be denied to you and me,
    Not having suffered their calamities.

*Under the patient glance of Evalkidas the guards
withdraw to stand in the background, as before.*

Kore: Evalkidas…in trying to help us
    You lost your life - that life that was a light
    For all the people.
Chorus leader: Had you been less great,
    You would not now be in this sorry state.
Evalkidas: For you I've only praise. I can't regret
    My having taken part in the revolt.
Chorus: The failed revolt…perhaps nothing, including
    Our own encounter, can be useful now.

*Ghost and chorus turn from each other. A flute player
begins a slow, haunting melody that seems to suggest
their thoughts and how these may develop.*
    *The ghost groans, as if riding awarenesses whose
depths gape below, sucking down much of his strength.
The chorus' own shrill cries blend with his to create a
misleadingly robust sound, like that of Spartan
bagpipes.*

Chorus: But tell us, if to speak of it is not
    Too hard for you, the course of your adventures,
    From that first day when, having disembarked
    At Koresos, you went to spend a while
    In Ephesos, preparing for your journey.

You prayed to Zeus, we know, and dipped your
   spears
In sacrificial blood, soldiers of far-flung
Cities, thus ceremonially united.
Evalkidas: Ionian joy was ours on those spring days...
   Naivety can shed old light on things;
   And fragmentary glimpses
   Find meanings, which mislead and yet have
     value...
   The household of a priestess took me in.
   'Let's not pretend,' she said. 'We both concede
   That it is not a bright idea to rejoice
   In what you've yet to achieve.' The following
     dawn
   The women in their shining clothes threw flowers
   Over our ranks as we were marching by.
   'You value freedom more than life,' they cried,
   'May you have both, young heroes!'
   We made our way by Kaystros' tranquil waters,
   And its reflected scenes, where nothing is
   Quite true or false, and all that is, is not;
   And nothing too bad ever really happens.
   Some of the men expressed to me their craving
   To be transferred into a world like that.
   'Evalkidas - our arbiter of things
   In general, please grant our wish,' they said.
   Indeed I am your general, I said...
   Thus bantering, while resting by the stream
   Among the willows, we would soothe our minds,
   Using imagined practicalities
   To offset real ones of this cruel world.
   'The Persians are not near at hand,' we heard
   From local men. 'You might approach and climb

The golden mountain if you choose.
Herakles guide you!'
For some days food was ours in plenty from
The ox carts sent with us from Ephesos.
We grew impatient, however, of their slowness,
And hurried forward, getting food by force
Or goodwill from the villages we passed.
On the fifth day, under a cloud of dust
We climbed some crude paths to the Pactolus,
That stream which swirls down gold so naively,
Oblivious of the fuss men make about it.
We dipped our helmets in, to have a drink.
'Better than gold is water,' we agreed.
Below us lay the urban sprawl of Sardis,
The capital of Lydia, where Croesus
Enjoyed abundant wealth, if not what you
And I call happiness.

Chorus leader: He may have been
    A vain and cruel despot, but his era
    Appears a better one by far than this.

Evalkidas: Across a deep ravine yet fairly close
    To us, being on a spur of Tmolus,
    Was the acropolis. Its old royal palace
    Would no doubt look much better if the Persians
    Had not constructed barracks right beside it.
    The lower town seemed rich but primitive.
    Darius' western capital appeared
    Some rustic place evolved to huge proportions.
    Those buildings were mostly of reeds and mud;
    And not even the few of brick or stone
    Were under our new-fangled tiles, but thatched.
    Our glances traced the narrow
    And labyrinthine streets, many of them

Perpetual strangers to intense sunlight;
Then, stretching far away, vineyards and fields
Of grain; apple and pomegranate trees,
Their early bloom a kind of gentle fire...
All seemed so orderly and admirable
Within the city and beyond it too.
An offering of first-fruits was in progress
Before Kybebe's temple...
That legendary region, opulent
And rich in confidence and *savoir vivre*,
Now clear to us at last, enchanted us.
Invisibly to those within the city
Our men quickly descended folds of Tmolus.
The trees obscured us as we neared the walls -
Still no alarm was raised. Those walls were in
A poor condition, and supported ivy,
Its loops - the gift, it seemed, of Dionysos -
Our handholds as we climbed and leapt across.
Some fruit trees swaying in the breeze; and houses
Still warm from spirits of the absent, who
Thought soon to return from the festival,
Received us (so we felt) hospitably.
Like illnesses which fly upon the air
We spread, progressed. The men and women
    whom
I passed, I informed: 'This is a joyous day!'
The abusive words, the cries and screams, the blare
Of trumpets soon gave way almost to quiet.
The fine economy, losing coherence,
Gave way to no unanimous resistance
Of soldiery and citizens together;
But men ran here and there towards their homes.
I imagine there to have been some violence.

If so, I never saw it. 'We have such power
As saves us from the need to kill,' we noted.
The townsmen seemed to feign their own absence.
But we could feel upon us many glances
From rooms that overlooked our nonchalance.
At leisure and almost sightseers (but seers
We were not - or if so, seers of illusion)
We looked forward to seizing grain and wine,
Fine robes and treasures wrought in gold and
   silver.
Our heralds - men of Ephesos whose dialect
Was most familiar in this locality -
Went here and there announcing the alliance
That would or should or might be made between
Us and the citizens. Some high class folk
Spoke down to us from windows of the main
   street;
And elsewhere too some dialogues began
Between the outraged Sardians and ourselves.
But meanwhile, close to me, a brand was hurled.
It rested on some thatch. The god of fire
Whom Persians worship so assiduously,
Set briskly to his work. Some of our men
Began to laugh and sing. 'We're like those
   Greeks,'
They cried, 'who stole along the streets of Troy
And burnt that city down!' As, all around,
House after flimsy house received the god
And started to collapse, our hopes of gain
Caved in and perished too. Even before this
We'd got the impression that the citizens
Were none too keen to enter the alliance.
They said things more or less to this effect:

'To evince trust and meekness towards our masters
Is most helpful...' 'They laugh, despise us and,
Being pleased to witness our subservience,
Also reward us, safeguarding our wellbeing.
But you, who break the Persian peace, assume
We see this war as useful to ourselves.
We don't!' Our reasoning was met with looks
Of fear, bewilderment, incomprehension...
We claimed to have thought better of the Sardians.
Some said the brand was tossed, the fire started,
To punish Lydian attitudes. But really
It was a mere caprice, a fatal whim.
We gathered where the river Pactolus
Flows through some open ground - their market
  place,
I think it was. The citizens could not
But congregate nearby, and Persians too
We saw among them as a ring of fire,
Much taller than the structures it devoured,
Asserted its magnificence and power
And made us seem a gathering of friends,
United in our fear. Meanwhile from far
Within the inferno screams arose from those
Who could find no way out. A few ran through
The flames to leap into the Pactolus.
They might emerge, bloodied and crying out,
Before being wrestled to the ground by pain
And injuries that took away their strength.
The worst afflicted seemed most fortunate,
As kindly Death received them to himself.
'The town is ours,' we claimed, as Sardians
Threw stones or struck contemptuously at our
  shields.

'What town?' they said, more in dismay than
   anger.
And then they laughed and pointed to the place
Hard by the temple where the Royal Road
Begins. 'Just follow it,' they taunted us,
'And in two months, or three, you'll be in Susa,
Or great Persepolis. Try burning that!'
A mile or so distant, towards the east,
The citadel on its sheer cliffs remained
Aloof, remote from flames which made it glow
More brightly than the shrouded evening sun.
Up there the Satrap, Artaphernes, waited.
(For you will understand, the acropolis
Was never ours. - It's almost in the heavens,
Precipitous, impregnable, and safe.)
The fitful charges of the Sardians
Perhaps were meant to goad us into staying.
'You do well to gain merit in the eyes
Of Artaphernes!' we cried out to them.
Our spies began to signal from mount Tmolus
That barbarian help was on its way.
We could not keep the scales upon our eyes,
But slunk along the valley of the stream,
Some holding up their shields against the heat
As they went by the blazing, falling buildings.
When we looked back in darkness from high
   ground
The temple of Kybebe seemed to show
In subtle fiery tongues of green and turquoise
How fine her precious offerings once were.
'We may not have it in us to survive
The aftermath of what we did today.'
I hear such sayings as we seek refuge

Upon the mountain; sullen silences
Then fall as we retreat the way we came.
To advance further would be suicidal.
But to return is certainly not safe.
We reach the Kaystros valley. Every step
Might lead into an ambush; and the sounds
And shadows seem to threaten eerily.
No pause that night and little the next day
From rapid flight. Melanthios, who commands
The Athenians, wrings his hands and says to me,
'If only we'd been less bold and heroic!'
Meanwhile our men are cursing him and me
For all the things we said while still at home
In favour of this fatal expedition.
I don't defend myself; why waste my strength?
And then again, I feel they are not wrong.
The general of Ionia, Charopinos
(A name we tend to abbreviate to Charon,
In reference to that surly ferryman
Of spirits of the dead) has talked things over
With friends of his. They've taken our few horses
And ridden off, perhaps to Ephesos.
He spoke on leaving of his further plans.
'To bring about some more catastrophes
No doubt!' is our general response to his
Reported words. At evening we rest.
We sleep till deep into the night, no lamps
Burning. We take for granted that
We're being pursued, but in the next few days
We march on slowly, doggedly, without
The haste we used at first. We are
A famine not of nutriment but meaning,
The cries of our own victims echoing

Within our minds. Those were not troops we had
  killed,
But men, women, children, the newly born...
And if some of the men indeed were soldiers,
Or had been at some time, it seems to us
They qualify for re-categorization.
We say it's not our fault, at least not in
The worst sense... In some dawn we note how
  rays
Flash intermittently from shields and weapons,
Accoutrements of horsemen...who hold off
To wait, we assume, for infantry support.
No doubt much of the region now is roused
To our perdition. Glancing west we see
Sunlight reflected on the tranquil waves.
'The afternoon's the time for rest,' I say
Sardonically, under the midday sun.
The angry faces of the enemy
Become quite clear. The walls of Ephesos
Are in a sea-mist shroud; but to our left
The Artemis temple and precinct, though low
  lying,
Escape the obscurity. 'Our safety seems
To taunt, not beckon us.' (So I reflect.)
'Some dreamer might suspect diviner realms
Were easier of access than the town.'
I get our men to form in readiness
For battle. Our war-chant drowns cries of
  stragglers,
And seems an added cruelty, as if
We hardly wish to know that they're in trouble.
What prowess we retain we hardly use,
So many of us fall as missiles find

Bare flesh or pierce their armour.

                              Suddenly,
As searing pain afflicts my head, my hand
Fails to obey. I've felt a crack of bone,
An impetus, a shaft that's buried deep.
My friends begin to draw behind the lines
This thing that once was me. Sight drowns in
   blood.
Then Sleep and Death benumb and end my pain
- My pain of body, that is, not of soul.
For anguish of the soul remains forever.
What remedy could such defeat receive?

But tell me what occurred after my death
And the withdrawal of the Athenians.
It's not that I know little of these things -
But it would interest me to hear how others
Have viewed events that I can hardly face.
Chorus: Many Athenians, as you imply,
Escaping from the carnage, reached their ships
And sailed for home. Whatever woeful tales
Melanthios and the others might bring back
We thought would be a spur to greater daring.
We thought that further help would be
   forthcoming,
That Athens was committed to our side.
So revolution spread from town to town.
Byzantium joined us, and the seaport Kaunos,
And other towns of Karia besides.
For five more years the great revolt continued.

The courage of our men brought such rewards
As loss, destruction, pain…and lasting pride
In things that evanesced before their eyes.
No further help has reached us from the cities
Which colonised our land in former ages.
For our misguided faith we are well-punished.
Our city of Miletos has been stormed,
Our most attractive youths are now eunuchs,
Dispersed among the harems of the east;
Our husbands dead, and we bereft foresee
A life of slavery and misery.
Our land is ours no more. Where will we be
Tomorrow? We don't know. We hate our
    masters;
Their pride is in their inhumanity.

*Enter on the wall, a figure in a white robe. On his head
is a crown of golden bay leaves. His speech is
recitative at first, the flute-player playing a slow
melody. The god is not noticed by the guards.*

Apollo: Abandoning my shrine at Didyma,
    Which now is just a burnt-out ruin, I,
    Apollo, son of Zeus, have come to view
    The place which once supplied its wealth and
        splendour.
    Unconscious irony is in the smiles
    Of those demure and confident young maidens
    Who, carved in stone, adorn the lower part
    Of columns there. Survivors of Miletos,

(The flute player falls silent.)

See why I would not back this great revolt!
I said where it would lead, I warned you all.
Your punishment, if not just, is decreed.
Now you will wash the feet of long-haired men,
Your city being their banquet and their spoil;
And I too have my troubles to endure,
Losing my finest Asiatic shrine.
While dwelling in your grief and anguish where
The Tigris meets the sea, you should address
Some prayers to me and Nemesis, and think
Of Sparta, Athens, Syracuse, Corcyra,
And other places which as yet are free.
Be happy in the happiness of others!
Thus balancing your thoughts you'll stave off
    madness.
But you should know you never will again
Look on your homes. All's lost forever, here.

(He turns to address the ghost.)

You are yourself, Evalkidas, no change
Bereaving you of authenticity
Is asked of you.
Your life and aspirations will revive.
Evalkidas: Great Lord Apollo, I have carefully
    Weighed in my mind your prophecies,
    And then ignored them.
Apollo: They're not a list
    Of things that I approve of or admire.
    Had you not disregarded my own words
    I would respect you less.
Evalkidas: The spring of youth returns for me at last...

Apollo: Indeed, as when at the Isthmian games
　　You won your famous victories
　　As runner and as charioteer.
Evalkidas: During the feasting there I poured libations
　　To spirits from the past, the heroes who,
　　I said, 'look on and help to guide us all
　　Towards a deeper sense of love and meaning
　　And purpose in ephemeral events.'
Apollo: Now you, Evalkidas, are such a spirit.
　　Your psyche is a fire; the gods revere you.
　　You are a great Daimon, and may inspire
　　The souls of men to seek a better course,
　　Abhorring all the ways of barbarism.
　　You may instil into Darius' dreams
　　A deepening disquiet; or then again
　　Prefer to leave him in his arrogance,
　　Rather than try on him your own free thoughts.
　　Why would he let go hubris if it seems
　　To him to be a proof that he's divine?
　　You'll foster in your countrymen a sense
　　Of common interest in unity.
　　But come, Evalkidas; yes, come to me.

*Evalkidas ascends 'steps' of the dilapidated wall to join
the god, who puts his arm round the hero's shoulder.
Exeunt Apollo and Evalkidas.*

*　　Members of the chorus look on stupefied as god and
hero leave. The women exchange glances and raise
their heads in a negative gesture as they reflect on their
non-Hellenic non-destiny. The women look at their
guards from time to time, and they at them.*

Some higher ranking soldiers enter.

First soldier:

> *(to the women and children; his first word showing*
> *that he has momentarily forgotten that they don't*
> *understand Persian. The second syllable of Yauna,*
> *which means 'Ionians' in his own language, is*
> *long.)*

Yauna, you must leave now. You have been
    spared.
Second soldier:
    You have a few months' journey ahead of you.
First soldier: Darius, King of kings presides over
    A prosperous empire, and the Tigris valley,
    Your new home, is the heart of civilisation.
Second soldier: There people behave well...
One of the guards:
            ...
        ...unlike you Greeks!
Second soldier:
    Well, you will change, perhaps, adapt to our
    culture.
    But don't worry, you can still speak Greek if
    You want. I know our language can be difficult.
First soldier: You'll find we will inflict no further
    harm
    On you or on your children. Come, this way.

*The Chorus and their children are moved on by the
guards. The younger, more recalcitrant women have
their hands tied and are pulled along by force.*

Chorus leader (turning to look back at the audience):
    Darius pities Greece, when he imagines
    She might miss out on his *Pax Persica,*
    And what he sees as its great benefits!

*Exeunt all except three soldiers. These, from among the
most recently arrived, are of quite high class as their
clothes reveal. (The most expensive of the colours they
wear is the saffron yellow.) They tend to have an easy
(we do own the place) manner. But of the three, the
Second Persian is the least sure of himself. He more
affects than shares the easy manner of the others.
Before they begin to sit around on rocks, the first
Persian pats him on the back, apparently to encourage
his progress to a more manly and soldierly confidence.*

First Persian (reassuringly):
    One of their gods - Apollo, son of Zeus -
    Has foretold *their* defeats, *our* victories.
Second Persian:
    This is the god whose shrine is now in flames
    At Didyma?
First Persian: Oh yes, the very same.
    Don't fear the coming wars; don't be disturbed.
    We will win easily.
    The Greeks will soon exemplify a charming
    And sane simplicity, in servitude.
    Soon it will be the case that the old Greek values
    Can't be corrupted, having evanesced.

Third Persian: For once the values are no longer there,
 But are abandoned, they can never be
 In any way perverted or damaged.
First Persian: Our allies seem more numerous each
 time
 We try and assess how many they may be.
Second Persian: The golden age of servitude has yet
 To dawn for Greece. The official whom we call
 The King's Eye's well aware they've far to go
 Before they come to accept our dominance.
First Persian: That's so, but wait and see..
Third Persian: The very thought of obtaining the
 approval
 Of the Great King is bliss - as you and I
 Have often said.
First Persian: We have so much to give...
Third Persian: We may not punish the Athenians after
 all
 For what they did to Sardis - it depends
 On whether they behave themselves in future.
 For like our armour with its glinting scales,
 Our wise approach is multi-faceted,
 Death, money and kindness being all on offer.
First Persian: Our power will be a great display, a
 pageant,
 Prepared for war, indeed; but you will find
 The coming struggle's nothing to write home
 About; and that it rivals in its lack
 Of incident and violence even
 Our altercations with the Babylonians,
 Who quickly became sheep under our guidance.
Third Persian: My friend, be confident. You will not
 have

To die to prove yourself worthy to live!
The expensive blue and saffron that you'll wear
To Greece will not be stained with your own
    blood.

First Persian: This day's special. So let us now
    proclaim
And celebrate before pure Anahita
And the other gods whom Zarathustra honoured
How war is or soon will be of the past.

Third Persian (in a low voice):
I think some good reports may reach the King,
And things we've said might well win us
    promotion
If we are being spied on at this moment.

Second Persian: Oh may it be that lasting peace *has*
    come,
And we can live in pleasure from now on!

Exeunt

Chronological Notes

546: Fall of Sardis to forces of Cyrus of Persia.
Peisistratos begins his third reign as tyrant of Athens.
536, 532, 528: In these years Kimon son of Stesagoras
is victorious in the chariot racing at Olympia.
528: Death of Peisistratos; accession of his son
Hippias; assassination of Kimon.
521: Here Miltiades son of Kimon is assumed, in the
novel, to marry the elder daughter of Hippias. Miltiades
and Euphrosyne will have two children: Glaukothea
and Metiochos.
516: Miltiades is sent by Hippias to govern the
Chersonese (i.e. the Gallipoli peninsula).
514: Murder of Hipparchos, brother of Hippias.
513: Under the leadership of their King Darius, the
Persians (or 'Medes' as they are often called in Athens)
cross over, in considerable force, into Europe. They
invade Scythia (north of the Ister, or Danube).
Miltiades' advice to his fellow tyrants, who are with
him at the Ister, is to break the bridge of boats. From
now on he will be considered an enemy by Darius.
512: Hippias sends his younger daughter, Archedike, to
marry Aiantides, son of Hippoklos tyrant of Lampsakos
(on the Asiatic side of the Hellespont). (Thus Hippias
seems to be making a pro-Persian alliance.) Miltiades
withdraws to the court of king Olorus of Thrace.
510: Fall of the tyranny at Athens.
508: Kleisthenes offers the Athenians a democratic
constitution, which they accept.

508-6: Spartan attempts are being made against the democracy.

503: In the novel, Miltiades is assumed to return to Athens with his new family, around this time. He is now married to Hegesipyle, daughter of Olorus of Thrace.

499: Ionian revolt. Miltiades returns to Chersonese.

495: According to the novel, his daughters Gaukothea, Elpinike and Kallidike sail to Athens, the Chersonese no longer being considered safe.

494: Fall of Miletos; end of the revolt.

493: In the spring, Miltiades escapes to Athens, but his son Metiochos is captured by the Phoenician fleet. Miltiades is put on trial on a charge of 'tyranny in the Chersonese'.

491: Persian envoys arrive in Athens to request symbols of submission.

490: Battle of Marathon.

489: Second trial of Miltiades. He is condemned for making a misleading public statement, and dies soon afterwards in prison.